Also by Louis Sachar

The Cardturner

Holes
Small Steps
Stanley Yelnats' Survival Guide to Camp Green Lake

For Younger Readers

Marvin Redpost series

Dogs Don't Tell Jokes
The Boy Who Lost His Face
There's a Boy in the Girls' Bathroom

LOUIS SACHAR

FUZZY MUD

WITHDRAWN

Delacorte Press

Text copyright © 2015 by Louis Sachar
Jacket art copyright © 2015 by Jeff Nentrup
Map copyright © 2015 by Jeffery Mathison

All rights reserved. Published in the United States by Delacorte Press,
an imprint of Random House Children's Books, a division of Random House LLC,
a Penguin Random House Company, New York.

Delacorte Press is a registered trademark and the colophon
is a trademark of Random House LLC.

Visit us on the Web! randomhousekids.com

Educators and librarians, for a variety of teaching tools, visit us at
RHTeachersLibrarians.com

Library of Congress Cataloging-in-Publication Data
Sachar, Louis.
Fuzzy mud / Louis Sachar.
pages cm
ISBN 978-0-385-74378-5 (trade hardcover) —
ISBN 978-0-375-99129-5 (library binding) — ISBN 978-0-385-37021-9 (ebook)
[1. Diseases—Fiction. 2. Schools—Fiction.] I. Title.
PZ7.S1185Fu 2015
[Fic]—dc23
2014025074

The text of this book is set in 12-point Apollo.
Book design by Trish Parcell

Printed in the United States of America
10 9 8 7 6 5 4 3 2 1
First Edition

Random House Children's Books
supports the First Amendment and celebrates the right to read.

*To Carla, for putting up
with all my idiosyncrasies
and foibles*

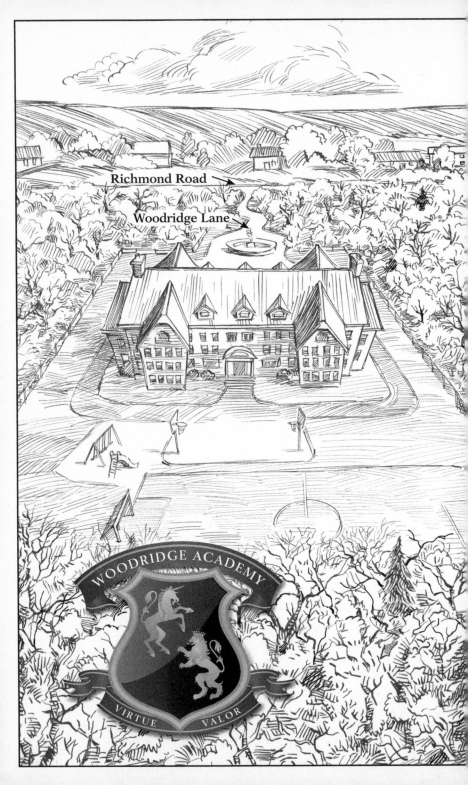

Richmond Road

Woodridge Lane

WOODRIDGE ACADEMY

VIRTUE   VALOR

1

Woodridge Academy, a private school in Heath Cliff, Pennsylvania, had once been the home of William Heath, after whom the town had been named. Nearly three hundred students now attended school in the four-story, black-and-brown stone building where William Heath had lived from 1891 to 1917, with only his wife and three daughters.

Tamaya Dhilwaddi's fifth-grade classroom on the fourth floor had been the youngest daughter's bedroom. The kindergarten area had once been the stables.

The lunchroom used to be a grand ballroom, where elegantly dressed couples had sipped champagne and danced to a live orchestra. Crystal chandeliers still hung from the ceiling, but these days the room permanently smelled of stale macaroni and cheese. Two hundred and eighty-nine kids, ages five to fourteen, crammed their mouths with Cheetos, made jokes about boogers, spilled milk, and shrieked for no apparent reason.

Tamaya didn't shriek, but she did gasp very quietly as she covered her mouth with her hand.

"He's got this superlong beard," a boy was saying, "splotched all over with blood."

"And no teeth," another boy added.

They were boys from the upper grades. Tamaya felt excited just talking to them, although, so far, she had been too nervous to actually say anything. She was sitting in the middle of a long table, eating lunch with her friends Monica, Hope, and Summer. One of the older boys' legs was only inches away from hers.

"The guy can't chew his own food," said the first boy. "So his dogs have to chew it up for him. Then they spit it out, and then he eats it."

"That is so disgusting!" exclaimed Monica, but from the way her eyes shone when she said it, Tamaya could tell that her best friend was just as excited as she was to have the attention of the older boys.

The boys had been telling the girls about a deranged hermit who lived in the woods. Tamaya didn't believe half of what they said. She knew boys liked to show off. Still, it was fun to let herself get caught up in it.

"Except they're not really dogs," said the boy sitting next

to Tamaya. "They're more like wolves! Big and black, with giant fangs and glowing red eyes."

Tamaya shuddered.

Woodridge Academy was surrounded by miles of woods and rocky hills. Tamaya walked to school every morning with Marshall Walsh, a seventh-grade boy who lived three houses down from her and on the other side of their tree-lined street. Their walk was almost two miles long, but it would have been a lot shorter if they hadn't had to circle around the woods.

"So what does he eat?" asked Summer.

The boy next to Tamaya shrugged. "Whatever his wolves bring him," he said. "Squirrels, rats, people. He doesn't care, just so long as it's food!"

The boy took a big bite of his tuna fish sandwich, then imitated the hermit by curling his lips so that it looked like he didn't have any teeth. He opened and closed his mouth in an exaggerated manner, showing Tamaya his partially chewed food.

"You are so gross!" exclaimed Summer from the other side of Tamaya.

All the boys laughed.

Summer was the prettiest of Tamaya's friends, with straw-colored hair and sky-blue eyes. Tamaya figured that was probably the reason the boys were talking to them in the first place. Boys were always acting silly around Summer.

Tamaya had dark eyes and dark hair that hung only

halfway down her neck. It used to be a lot longer, but three days before school started, while she was still in Philadelphia with her dad, she made the drastic decision to chop it off. Her dad took her to a very posh hair salon that he probably couldn't afford. As soon as she got it cut, she was filled with regret, but when she got back to Heath Cliff, her friends all told her how mature and sophisticated she looked.

Her parents were divorced. She spent most of the summer with her dad, and one weekend each month during the school year. Philadelphia was on the opposite end of the state, three hundred miles away. When she returned home to Heath Cliff, she always had the feeling that she'd missed something important while she'd been gone. It might have been nothing more than an inside joke that her friends all laughed at, but she always felt a little left out, and it took her a while to get back into the groove.

"He came *this close* to eating me," said one of the boys, a tough-looking kid with short black hair and a square face. "A wolf snapped at my leg just as I was climbing back over the fence."

The boy stood on top of the bench and showed the girls his pant leg for proof. It was covered in dirt, and Tamaya could see a small hole just above his sneaker, but that could have come from anything. Besides, she thought, if he'd been running *away* from the wolf, then the hole would have been in the back of his pants, not the front.

The boy stared down at her. He had blue, steel-like eyes, and Tamaya got the feeling that he could read her mind and was daring her to say something.

She swallowed, then said, "You're not really allowed in the woods."

The boy laughed, and then the other boys laughed too.

"What are you going to do?" he challenged. "Tell Mrs. Thaxton?"

She felt her face redden. "No."

"Don't listen to her," said Hope. "Tamaya's a real Goody Two-shoes."

The words stung. Just a few seconds earlier, she had been feeling so cool, talking with the older boys. Now they were all looking at her as if she were some kind of freak.

She tried making a joke out of it. "I guess I'll only wear one shoe from now on."

Nobody laughed.

"You are kind of a goody-goody," said Monica.

Tamaya bit her lip. She didn't get why what she had said had been so wrong. After all, Monica and Summer had just called the boys *disgusting* and *gross,* but somehow that was okay. If anything, the boys seemed proud that the girls thought they were disgusting and gross.

When did the rules change? she wondered. *When did it become bad to be good?*

• • •

Across the lunchroom, Marshall Walsh sat amid a bunch of kids, all laughing and talking loudly. On one side of Marshall sat one group. On his other side sat a different group. Between these two groups, Marshall silently ate alone.

2

SunRay Farm

In a secluded valley thirty-three miles northwest of Woodridge Academy was SunRay Farm. You wouldn't know it was a farm if you saw it. There were no animals, no green pastures, and no crops—at least, none that grew big enough for anyone to see with the naked eye.

Instead, what you would see—if you made it past the armed guards, past the electric fence topped with barbed wire, past the alarms and security cameras—would be rows and rows of giant storage tanks. You also wouldn't be able to see the network of tunnels and underground pipes connecting the storage tanks to the main laboratory, also underground.

Hardly anyone in Heath Cliff knew about SunRay Farm, and certainly not Tamaya or her friends. Those who had heard of it had only vague ideas about what was going on there. They might have heard of Biolene but probably didn't know exactly what it was.

A little more than a year before—that is, about a year before Tamaya Dhilwaddi cut her hair and started the fifth grade—the United States Senate Committee on Energy and the Environment held a series of secret hearings regarding SunRay Farm and Biolene.

The following testimony is excerpted from that inquiry:

SENATOR WRIGHT: You worked at SunRay Farm for two years before being fired, is that correct?

DR. MARC HUMBARD: No, that is not correct. They never fired me.

SENATOR WRIGHT: I'm sorry. I'd been informed—

DR. MARC HUMBARD: Well, they may have tried to fire me, but I'd already quit. I just hadn't told anyone yet.

SENATOR WRIGHT: I see.

SENATOR FOOTE: But you no longer work there?

DR. MARC HUMBARD: I couldn't be in the same room with Fitzy a minute longer! The man's crazy. And when I say *crazy*, I mean one hundred percent bananas.

SENATOR WRIGHT: Are you referring to Jonathan Fitzman, the inventor of Biolene?

DR. MARC HUMBARD: Everyone thinks he's some kind of genius, but who did all the work? Me, that's who! Or at least, I would have, if he had let me. He'd pace around the lab, muttering to himself, his arms flailing. It was impossible for the rest of us to concentrate. He'd sing songs! And if you asked him to stop, he'd look at you like you were the one who was crazy! He wouldn't even know he was singing. And then, out of the blue, he'd slap the side of his head and shout, "No, no, no!" And suddenly I'd have to stop everything I'd been working on and start all over again.

SENATOR WRIGHT: Yes, we've heard that Mr. Fitzman can be a bit . . . eccentric.

SENATOR FOOTE: Which is one reason why we are concerned about Biolene. Is it truly a viable alternative to gasoline?

SENATOR WRIGHT: This country needs clean energy, but is it safe?

DR. MARC HUMBARD: Clean energy? Is that what they're calling it? There's nothing clean about it. It's an abomination of nature! You want to know what they're doing at SunRay Farm? You really want to know? Because I know. I know!

SENATOR FOOTE: Yes, we want to know. That's why you've been called before this committee, Mr. Humbard.

DR. MARC HUMBARD: Doctor.

SENATOR FOOTE: Excuse me?

DR. MARC HUMBARD: It's "Dr. Humbard," not "Mr. Humbard." I have a PhD in microbiology.

SENATOR WRIGHT: Our apologies. Tell us, please, Dr. Humbard, what are they doing at SunRay Farm that you find so abominable?

DR. MARC HUMBARD: They have created a new form of life, never seen before.

SENATOR WRIGHT: A kind of high-energy bacteria, as I understand it. To be used as fuel.

DR. MARC HUMBARD: Not bacteria. Slime mold. People always confuse the two. Both are microscopic, but they are really quite different. We began with simple slime mold, but Fitzy altered its DNA to create something new: a single-celled living creature that is totally unnatural to this planet. SunRay Farm is now growing these man-made microorganisms—these tiny Frankensteins—so that they can burn them alive inside automobile engines.

SENATOR FOOTE: Burn them alive? Don't you think that's a bit strong, Dr. Humbard? We're talking about microbes here. After all, every time I wash my hands or brush my teeth, I kill hundreds of thousands of bacteria.

DR. MARC HUMBARD: Just because they're small doesn't mean their lives aren't worthwhile. SunRay Farm is creating life for the sole purpose of destroying it.

SENATOR WRIGHT: But isn't that what all farmers do?

3

After school, Tamaya waited by the bike racks for Marshall. The racks were empty. Most of the students at Woodridge Academy lived too far away to ride their bikes, and there were no school buses for the private school. A line of cars extended from the circular driveway up Woodridge Lane toward Richmond Road.

As Tamaya watched the other kids climb into cars and drive off, she wished she had a ride too. She was already dreading the long walk home. It would feel even longer with a backpack full of books.

Her face still burned with shame every time she thought about what had happened in the lunchroom. She was mad at Hope for saying what she'd said, and even madder at

Monica, who was supposed to be her best friend and who should have stuck up for her.

So she was a good girl? *So what?* What was wrong with that?

Being good was partly what Woodridge Academy was all about. The students all wore school uniforms: khaki pants and blue sweaters for boys, plaid skirts and maroon sweaters for girls. Embroidered on each sweater, right under the name of the school, were the words *Virtue and Valor*.

Besides learning about history and math and all that, the students at Woodridge Academy were also learning to be *virtuous*. The school was supposed to teach them how to be good people. When Tamaya was in the second grade, she had to memorize a list of ten virtues: charity, cleanliness, courage, empathy, grace, humility, integrity, patience, prudence, and temperance. This year, she was learning their synonyms and antonyms.

But if you actually tried to be good, Tamaya thought bitterly, everyone acted like you were some kind of freak!

Marshall came out of the building. His hair was a mess, and his sweater, stretched out of shape, seemed to hang crookedly.

She didn't wave. He came toward her, then trudged on past with hardly a glance.

Marshall had a rule. They weren't supposed to act like friends around school. They were just two kids who walked to school together because *they had to*. They definitely were not boyfriend and girlfriend, and Marshall didn't want anyone thinking they were.

Tamaya was surprised, however, because he wasn't going the usual way. Normally they headed up Woodridge Lane and then turned right on Richmond Road. Instead, Marshall was heading toward the side of the school.

She adjusted her backpack, then caught up to him.

"Where are you going?"

"Home," he said, as if she'd just asked a really stupid question.

"But—"

"I'm taking a shortcut," he snapped.

That didn't make any sense. They'd walked the same way every single day for the last three years. How could he suddenly know a shortcut?

He continued around the side of the school toward the back. He was taller than she was, and was walking quickly. Tamaya struggled to keep up. "How do you suddenly know a shortcut?" she asked.

He stopped and turned on her. "I don't *suddenly* know about it," he told her. "I've known about it my whole life."

That didn't make any sense either.

"If you want to take the slow way home, that's up to you," Marshall said. "No one's making you come with me."

That wasn't really true, and he knew it. Her mother didn't allow her to walk home alone.

"I'm going with you, aren't I?" Tamaya said.

"Well, then quit being a baby about it," said Marshall.

She stayed with him as he crossed the blacktop, then went out onto the soccer field. All she'd done was ask how he knew a shortcut, she thought. How was that "being a baby"?

Marshall kept glancing behind him. Every time he looked back, Tamaya instinctively did too, but she didn't see anything or anybody.

Tamaya still remembered her first day at Woodridge. She'd been in the second grade, and Marshall had been in the fourth. He had helped her find her classroom, pointed out where the girls' bathroom was, and personally introduced her to Mrs. Thaxton, the headmistress. The new school had seemed like a big, scary place to her, and Marshall had been her guide and protector.

She'd had a secret crush on him all through second, third, and fourth grades. Maybe it still lingered a little bit inside her, but lately he'd been acting like such a jerk, she wasn't sure she even liked him anymore.

Beyond the soccer field, the ground sloped down unevenly toward the chain-link fence that separated the schoolyard from the woods. As they moved closer to the fence, Tamaya could feel her heartbeat quicken. The air was cool and damp, but her throat felt dry and tight.

Just a few weeks before, the woods had sparkled with bright fall colors. Looking out the window from her classroom on the fourth floor, she'd been able to see every shade of red, orange, and yellow, so bright some days that it had looked as though the hillside were on fire. But now the colors had faded and the trees looked dark and gloomy.

She wished she could be as brave as Marshall. It wasn't just the woods that scared her—and what might or might not have been lurking within. Even more than that, Tamaya was scared to death of getting in trouble. Just the thought of a teacher yelling at her filled her heart with fear.

She knew that other kids broke the rules all the time, and nothing bad ever happened to them. Kids in her class would do something wrong, and then her teacher, Ms. Filbert, would tell them not to do it, and then they'd do it again the very next day and still not get in trouble.

Still, she was sure that if she went into the woods, something horrible would happen to her. Mrs. Thaxton might find out. She could get expelled.

A dip in the rocky ground created a gap big enough to crawl through under a section of the fence. Tamaya watched Marshall take off his backpack, then push it through the gap.

She took off her backpack too. Ms. Filbert had once said that courage just meant pretending to be brave. "After all, if you're not scared, then there's nothing to be brave about, is there?"

Pretending to be brave, Tamaya shoved her backpack through the gap. There was no turning back.

Now who's the goody-goody? she thought.

She wiggled under the fence, careful not to snag her sweater.

4

Marshall Walsh

Marshall Walsh wasn't as brave as Tamaya thought.

He used to have lots of friends. He used to like school. He had taken band in the sixth grade, and his music teacher, Mr. Rowan, had written on his report card that what he lacked in talent, he made up for with enthusiasm.

Marshall plays the tuba with gusto.

He wasn't enthusiastic about anything anymore. Each day brought him nothing but more misery and humiliation. And it had all started with a new kid in his class, Chad Hilligas.

Students attended Woodridge Academy for one of two reasons. Either they were really smart, or else their parents were really rich. Tamaya was one of the smart ones. Marshall was an in-betweener. His parents weren't rich, but they both had good jobs, and they considered education to be extremely important. They cut back in other areas, like family vacations and going out to restaurants.

The reason Chad Hilligas came to Woodridge was entirely different. He'd been kicked out of three schools in the last two years. The social worker assigned to his case believed that if he was placed in a more positive environment and made to wear a school uniform, he would stop fighting and become a more conscientious and motivated student. If his parents hadn't agreed to pay for him to go to Woodridge Academy, he would have been put in a school at a juvenile detention center.

So Chad had started with everyone else in September. The boys in Marshall's class were in awe of Chad. The girls seemed drawn to him too, even if he also scared them a little bit. And for the first few weeks of this year, Marshall had been right there with everyone else, hanging on every word Chad said, nodding along in agreement, laughing at his jokes.

Some people were terrified of being expelled from school. Chad bragged about it.

"My fourth-grade teacher kept giving me a hard time, so I locked her in the closet."

"What'd she do to you when she got out?"

"Nothing. She's still in there."

And Marshall had laughed right along with everyone else. Chad claimed he'd been kicked out of five schools, not just three. He was always coming up with new stories about things he had supposedly done. The more he got in trouble, the more everyone seemed to admire him.

Marshall remembered the moment Chad had turned against him. Chad had been telling about the time he had ridden his motorcycle to school.

"Did anyone see you?" Gavin asked.

"Yeah, they saw me," Chad replied. "I rode it right up the steps of the school and into the principal's office!"

"No way!" Marshall exclaimed.

Chad stopped talking and slowly turned to Marshall.

"You calling me a liar?"

Everyone became very quiet.

Marshall hadn't meant it that way at all. He just as easily could have exclaimed, "Awesome!"

"No."

"You all heard him," Chad said. "He called me a liar. Anybody else think I'm lying?"

Marshall tried to explain, but Chad shredded his feeble words with a cold, hard stare.

For the rest of the day, that stare seemed to follow Marshall wherever he went. And for what seemed like no logical reason to Marshall, slowly but surely, everyone else seemed to turn against him too.

"Whose side are you on?" Chad would ask. "You're either with me or you're with Buttface."

At first, Marshall tried to pretend that nothing was wrong.

He'd walk right up to a group of his friends and try to join in whatever they were doing, but one glance from Chad would send him away, his eyes cast down in shame.

Snide whispers followed him wherever he went, along with not-so-accidental bumps in the hallways. He became afraid to speak up in class. His grades got worse. Often when taking a test, he could feel Chad's stare burning through the back of his neck, and his mind would go blank.

In other schools, where seventh-grade students changed classrooms every period, Marshall and Chad might have had only one or two classes together. There were only forty-one seventh graders at Woodridge, however, and it was Marshall's bad luck that Chad was in every one of his classes except his last period, Latin.

Marshall had a brother and sister, twins, who were four years old. Even when he'd had friends and lots to do, he'd always been happy to look after them when necessary, or even when it wasn't necessary. Daniela and Eric liked to pretend they were lions in the circus. They'd crouch on top of the kitchen barstools and growl, and Marshall would be the lion tamer.

Since losing his other friends, Marshall no longer liked playing with the twins either. It made him feel like a loser. When his parents questioned him about his bad grades, he blamed it on them. "How am I supposed to study when they're roaring at me all the time?"

It was the same with Tamaya. Everyone picked on him all

day at school, and now he took it out on the only person who was nice to him. He'd hear himself say mean things to her and hate himself for it, but he couldn't seem to stop.

As bad as it had been for Marshall lately, today it had gotten even worse. He'd answered a question in class, right after Chad had given the wrong answer.

Afterward, as he was heading up the stairs on his way to Latin, Chad grabbed him from behind, pulled him down three steps, and shoved him against the railing.

"Listen, Buttface, we need to settle this once and for all."

"Settle what?" Marshall tried.

"After school, on the corner of Woodridge and Richmond Road," Chad told him. "And you better be there, you thumb-sucking coward."

Marshall and Tamaya always walked right past that corner on their way home. They'd been going the same way every day for three years. But today, he suddenly knew a shortcut.

5

By the time Tamaya made it to the other side of the fence, Marshall had already disappeared through the trees. She picked up her backpack and hurried after him, slipping her arms through the straps as she ran. Ducking under a low branch, she spotted him climbing over a small mound of boulders. "Wait up!" she called.

Again, he disappeared from view.

Her knee banged against one of the boulders as she scrambled over the mound. He was waiting for her on the other side, hands on hips, an annoyed look on his face. "What's the point in taking a shortcut if I have to keep stopping and waiting for you to come pokeying along?"

"I'm not pokeying," Tamaya insisted.

"Well, hurry up, then," said Marshall. He turned and started off again.

She stuck close to him as they followed a path that zigzagged through the trees. It had rained the night before, and damp leaves stuck to Tamaya's sneakers. Leaves continued to fall around them, one here, one there, gently drifting downward.

They must have missed a zig or a zag somewhere, because after a while it became clear to Tamaya that they were no longer on any kind of path. She had to fight her way through tangled branches and then step over a thick patch of thorny bushes.

"You think we should turn back?" she suggested.

Marshall's answer was short and blunt. "No."

Tamaya pretended to be brave. Every little noise made her heart leap. She got down on her hands and knees and crawled under a very low branch. "Is this the shortcut?" she asked as she straightened back up.

Marshall didn't answer. He just kept moving forward.

Her sock was torn, and her skirt was splotched with dirt. She didn't know how she'd explain that to her mother. One thing she couldn't do was lie. She would never lie to her mother.

Her parents had divorced back when she'd been in the first grade. They had been living in an apartment in Philadelphia at the time. It was a different apartment from the one her dad lived in now.

Even back then, everyone always talked about how smart she was, which had surprised her, because it wasn't something she gave much thought. She was who she was, and that was all. She'd been given an aptitude test, and then she and her mother had moved to Heath Cliff so she could attend Woodridge Academy.

One thing she wasn't smart about was her parents. She couldn't figure out why they'd separated and why they didn't just get back together. After the divorce her mother seemed very sad for a long time. On Tamaya's last visit to her father, he said to her, "You know I still love your mother very much. I always will." But when she repeated those words to her mother and suggested that maybe they should all live together again, her mother got all sad again.

"That will never happen," she told Tamaya.

Even now, as Tamaya was scared to death that she and Marshall might be lost in the woods *forever,* she couldn't help but think that maybe if she did get lost, her mom and dad would come looking for her *together*. She was imagining what it would be like when they found her, and how they'd all hug each other, when a small animal darted right in front of her.

She stopped. "What was that?" she asked Marshall.

"What was what?"

"You didn't see it?" She wondered if it could have been a fox. "Some kind of animal practically ran over my foot!"

"So?"

"So, nothing," she muttered. She didn't know why he was being so mean.

They came to an old dead tree lying on its side. Much of its bark had rotted away. Marshall climbed up on it and looked around. "Hmmm," he muttered. He looked back the way they had just come.

"Are we lost?" Tamaya asked.

"No," Marshall insisted. "I just need to get my bearings."

"You said you knew a shortcut!"

"I do," he answered. "I just have to find the exact place where it starts. Once I find the starting point, we'll be home in a snap." He snapped his fingers as if that proved it.

Tamaya waited. She heard something crackle behind her, but when she turned around, there was nothing there.

Marshall hopped down from the tree trunk. "This way!" he declared, as if he knew exactly where he was going.

Tamaya scooted around the tree and followed. She had no choice.

They made their way down the side of a hill until they came to a ravine, then followed the ravine upward. Tamaya's backpack felt heavier with every step. She kept thinking she heard something or someone behind her, but when she looked back, there was never anyone there.

Marshall continued to walk quickly. She constantly had to run to catch up but soon would lag behind again. Each time, it became harder to catch up.

Out of breath, she watched him disappear around a curve

in the hillside. She shifted the weight of her backpack, gathered what strength she had left, and started to run after him.

Something grabbed her from behind. She felt her sweater being pulled up against her neck, choking her.

She twisted free, then screamed as she fell to the ground. Rolling over, she looked up, but there was nobody—no deranged hermit, no bloodstained beard, just a tree limb with pointy branches.

Marshall came hurrying back down to her. "Are you okay?"

She felt more embarrassed than anything else. "I just fell," she said.

She realized her sweater must have gotten caught on the branch. That was all.

Marshall continued to look down at her. "I'm really sorry, Tamaya," he said finally.

He seemed really worried.

"I saw a rocky ledge up the hill," he told her. "You wait here. I'm going to climb up to it. I should be able to get a good view from up there."

"Don't leave me," she pleaded.

"I won't. I promise."

He took off his backpack and set it down next to her. "I'll be right back."

She watched him head back up the hill and disappear again around the curve. She took off her backpack and set it next to his. She was too worn out to follow.

She took off her sweater to see how badly it had been damaged. It was worse than she'd thought. There was a hole almost as big as her fist just above the right shoulder. She definitely didn't know how she'd explain that to her mother.

Even though she had been given a full scholarship to Woodridge, her mother still had to pay for the school uniform. The sweater had cost ninety-three dollars.

It wasn't fair.

She would never admit it to her friends, but she loved the school uniform. Monica, Hope, and Summer thought it made them look like dorks. They could go on and on about what they would wear on the last Friday of each month when they got to wear "real clothes." But Tamaya always felt proud to put on her sweater with the words *Virtue and Valor* written in gold, and the year 1924. It made her feel important, like she was a part of history.

As she was thinking about this, she found herself staring at a large puddle of some kind of fuzz-covered mud. Her mind barely registered it at first, but the more she gazed at the odd-looking mud, the more it drew her attention.

The mud was dark and tar-like. Just above the surface, almost as if it were suspended in midair, there was a fuzzy yellowish-brown scum.

Something else struck her as strange about the fuzzy mud, although it took her a moment to realize what it was. There were no leaves on top of the mud. Leaves had fallen everywhere else. They completely surrounded the mud puddle, right up to its edges, but for some reason, no leaves had landed on top of it.

She looked back up the hill. There was still no sign of Marshall.

Her gaze returned to the fuzzy mud. It was possible, she thought, that the leaves had sunk down into the mud, but the mud seemed too thick for a leaf to fall through it. She wondered if that fuzzy scum somehow swept the leaves off to the side.

A noise crackled from below. She turned toward the sound, and then heard it again. Something was moving through the trees.

She rose to one knee, ready to run, then caught a glimpse of someone wearing a blue sweater and khaki pants. It was the boys' school uniform.

She stood and waved her arms. "Hey!" she shouted.

The figure stopped.

"Over here!" she called.

As he came toward her, she recognized him as the boy who had sat next to her in the lunchroom. He was the one who had stood on the bench and said a wolf had bit a hole in his pant leg. She wasn't sure, but she thought his name might have been Chad.

She looked back up the hill and shouted, "Marshall! Marshall, we're saved!"

6

The Ergie

The following is another excerpt from the secret inquiry into SunRay Farm:

SENATOR WRIGHT: As I understand it, you invented Biolene while you were still in college?

JONATHAN FITZMAN: Well, not exactly. I got a C-minus on the paper I wrote about my idea for the ergie. So then I dropped out of college and continued to work on it in my parents' garage. They weren't too thrilled about that, if you know what I mean.

SENATOR WRIGHT: Mr. Fitzman, would you please try not to swing your arms so much as you answer our questions.

Jonathan Fitzman: Was I swinging my arms? Sorry. I have trouble sitting still too long. I think better when I'm moving.

Senator Wright: So what exactly is this *ergie* of yours?

Jonathan Fitzman: [*Laughs.*] That's just what I call the little guy. It's short for "ergonym." It's a single-celled, high-energy microorganism. Very intense! Totally awesome. I got a tattoo of one on my arm, if you want to see what it looks like. It's an exact replica.

Senator Foote: I can't see anything.

Senator March: Me neither.

Jonathan Fitzman: Well, like I said, it's an exact replica. [*Laughs.*] It's the smallest tattoo in the world! [*Laughs.*] You need an electron microscope to see it!

Senator Wright: And there are more than a million of these ergies in every gallon of Biolene?

Jonathan Fitzman: A million? Try a trillion. Or a quadrillion. Or, I don't know, what comes after that? A gazillion!

Senator Wright: Try to control your arms, Mr. Fitzman.

Jonathan Fitzman: Sorry. I don't even have a chair at my desk in my office. I have to keep moving.

Senator Foote: So you are no longer working out of your parents' garage?

Jonathan Fitzman: No, I've got this incredible laboratory now. My biology professor might not have thought much about the ergie, but some other folks did. Some very rich ones.

Senator Foote: How much does it cost SunRay Farm to produce one gallon of Biolene?

Jonathan Fitzman: I'm not the business guy. I'm the whadda-youcallit, the guy who thinks it all up and figures out how to do it. But I'd say the first gallon cost us somewhere around five hundred million dollars.

Senator Wright: Five hundred million dollars. And what about the second gallon?

Jonathan Fitzman: About nineteen cents.

7

TUESDAY, NOVEMBER 2
4:10 P.M.

"Be careful not to step in that," Tamaya warned as Chad Hilligas made his way around the strange mud. "What do you think all that weird fuzzy stuff is?" she asked.

She might as well have been speaking a foreign language, the way Chad looked at her. He spit on the ground, then looked her in the eye and demanded, "Where's Marshall?"

His tone was nasty, but Chad was her only hope, so she had to be nice to him. "He's climbing up on a ledge trying to find the way back home. We got lost. When I heard you coming, at first I thought you might have been that crazy hermit you were telling me about, but then I saw your blue sweater, so . . ." She shrugged and smiled.

Chad spit on the ground again, then walked past her,

heading after Marshall. He stopped as Marshall appeared from around the side of the hill.

Marshall hesitated just a second when he saw Chad, but then continued on down, as if nothing were the matter. "Hey, Chad," he said.

Tamaya sensed something was wrong. She could hear it in Marshall's voice.

"I waited for you," Chad said.

"I know," Marshall said. "I was on my way there, but then Tamaya said she knew a shortcut through the woods. What was I supposed to do? I have to walk home with her."

"My mom won't let me walk home alone," Tamaya explained.

Chad glanced at her, then turned back to Marshall. "You trying to make me feel like a fool, just standing there on the corner waiting for you?"

"No."

Chad stepped toward him, then pushed him backward. "You think I'm a fool, don't you?"

Marshall regained his balance. "No."

With sudden ferocity, Chad lunged at him. He slugged Marshall in the face, and then in the side of the neck.

Tamaya screamed.

Marshall tried to protect himself, but Chad hit him twice more, then grabbed him by the head and threw him to the ground.

"Leave him alone!" Tamaya shouted.

Chad glared at her. "You're next, Tamaya," he said.

Marshall tried to get up, but Chad's knee caught the side of his head, knocking him back down.

Tamaya didn't think. She just reacted.

She reached into the fuzzy mud and grabbed a handful of thick and gooey muck. She ran at Chad, and as he turned toward her, she shoved it into his face.

He lunged at her, but she was too quick, stepping to the side.

Chad stumbled past her, then bent over and covered his face with his hands.

For a moment, Tamaya was too scared to move.

Marshall scrambled to his feet. He grabbed both backpacks and shouted, "Run!"

Tamaya ran as hard as she could, for as long as she could, until it felt like her lungs would explode. She didn't know if Marshall had seen the way home or if they were running deeper into the woods. She didn't care, just so long as she got away from Chad.

She was still running when her foot caught in a tangle of vines, and the next thing she knew, she was sprawled across the dirt. Her heart pounded, and her hands stung from the fall. She took several long deep breaths as she tried to make herself get back up, but she just didn't have any strength left.

She was afraid to look behind her.

Marshall had stopped running after he'd heard her go

down. She saw him heading back toward her, still holding both backpacks. She could tell from the way he walked that Chad must not have been too close. She turned. Chad was nowhere to be seen.

She pushed herself up into a sitting position as Marshall approached.

"You okay?"

"I think so."

Her knees were scraped and bloody, and her left wrist hurt from when she'd fallen, but she didn't think there was anything seriously wrong. Besides, Marshall was a lot worse. Dried blood and snot was caked beneath his nose. Sweat dripped off his face.

"You think he's still coming?" she asked him.

"I don't know. But if not today, tomorrow."

Tamaya knew that was true. Chad's words still echoed inside her head. "You're next, Tamaya." And that was before she had smashed mud in his face.

She got back up to her feet and took her backpack from Marshall. They continued walking the way they had been going.

"Is this the way?" she asked. "Were you able to see anything from the ledge?"

"Not really," said Marshall.

"So what'd you do, anyway, to make him so mad?"

"I answered a question in class."

Tamaya didn't get it. "So?"

"It's different in the seventh grade. You're not supposed to act like you know anything."

The sky was beginning to turn dark. Tamaya worried that it wouldn't be long before they wouldn't be able to see anything.

"Look, smoke!" Marshall declared.

"Where?"

"It's smoke from a chimney," he told her.

She tried to follow where he was pointing, and then she saw it too, gray smoke against a gray sky.

They hurried toward it, although, for all Tamaya knew, it could have been coming from the home of the crazy hermit. She imagined them as Hansel and Gretel going to the home of the evil witch.

As they got closer to the source of the smoke, however, she saw that there wasn't just one isolated home but a whole street of houses, with parked cars and front lawns.

Tamaya stepped over a short metal barrier onto a road. She felt like getting down on her hands and knees and kissing the asphalt, but Marshall might have thought that was too weird.

She glanced back at a road sign that read DEAD END.

The streetlights came on as they were walking away from the woods. Tamaya suggested that they knock on somebody's door to see if they could get a ride home, but Marshall said they didn't need to. He knew the way. It wasn't too far.

Tamaya's right hand began to tingle, and she rubbed it with the other. It didn't exactly hurt. Her skin just felt sort of fizzy, like a freshly opened can of soda.

$$2 \times 1 = 2$$
$$2 \times 2 = 4$$

8

One Little Ergonym

The following is more of Jonathan Fitzman's testimony from the secret Senate hearings:

SENATOR MARCH: Excuse me, Mr. Fitzman, but I'm having a hard time getting my head wrapped around this. You said there are more than a trillion of your ergonyms in every gallon of Biolene.

JONATHAN FITZMAN: A lot more.

SENATOR MARCH: These are man-made organisms, right? So how could you possibly make that many?

JONATHAN FITZMAN: [*Laughs.*] You're right. That would be impossible. I had to make only one.

Senator March: I don't understand.

Jonathan Fitzman: One ergonym, capable of reproduction. That was the hardest part. That's what took me so long. The first few ergies I made were unable to survive the cell division process. The poor little fellows kept exploding.

Senator March: What do you mean, exploding?

Jonathan Fitzman: *Kaboom!* [*Laughs.*] In the lab, we can watch the images from the electron microscope projected onto a giant computer screen. It's quite cool. Every time one of my ergies got to the cell division stage—*kaboom!*—it looked like the Fourth of July.

Senator Wright: But eventually, I take it, you were able to create an ergonym that didn't explode?

Jonathan Fitzman: The perfect ergonym. It took two and a half years and five hundred million dollars, but we did it. One little ergie. And thirty-six minutes later, we had two. The second one was an exact copy of the first. And thirty-six minutes after that, four. Then eight. Then sixteen. Every thirty-six minutes, the population just keeps on doubling.

Senator March: Even so, to get the trillions of ergies you need for just one gallon of Biolene, it would take years.

Jonathan Fitzman: Not at all. Do the math. In twelve hours we had more than a million of the little guys, and by the next afternoon, more than a trillion. [*Sings.*] *One little, two little, three little ergonyms. Four little, five little, six little ergonyms.*

9

TUESDAY, NOVEMBER 2
5:48 P.M.

Weeds and clumps of grass poked through the cracks in the sidewalk. Tamaya crossed the street, sighed, then started up the wooden steps of her front porch. The middle step wobbled beneath her foot. Marshall's stupid shortcut had made her more than two hours late. Of course, she realized there never had been any shortcut, but that was the stupidest part about it. If he was afraid of Chad, he would have been safer walking along normal streets, with lots of people and cars around.

Her house was dark. Her mother occasionally worked late, and Tamaya hoped with all her heart that this was one of those days.

She wore her house key on a chain around her neck, but

when she reached for it, all she could feel was the empty chain. Filled with panic, she almost broke the chain as she tugged on it. Rotating it around her neck, she found the key.

She breathed a huge sigh of relief. Somehow it had twisted back behind her. Still, she knew her troubles were far from over.

She unlocked the door. "Hello?" she called as she opened it. "I'm home!"

There was no answer. So far, so good. No questions, no lies.

Tamaya switched on lights as she moved quickly through her house toward her bedroom. The rooms were smallish, and each was painted in bright bold colors; a red-and-blue kitchen, a yellow living room, a green hallway. Tamaya's room was turquoise with a yellow closet door and a yellow window frame. She dropped her backpack and collapsed onto the bed, but only for a moment.

Her right hand still felt all tingly. She went into the bathroom and examined it under the light. Tiny red bumps were sprinkled over her palm and fingers.

She washed with antibacterial soap and hot water—as hot as she could stand. Using a washcloth, she cleaned the dirt and blood off her arms and legs.

She was putting a Band-Aid on her knee when the phone rang. She wondered if her mother had been trying to call her for a long time. She rushed into her mother's bedroom and answered just before the fourth ring.

"Hello?"

"Hi, sweetie. Sorry I'm running so late."

"That's okay," she said. Guilt pumped through her veins.

"How does pizza sound to you?"

"Good."

"You all right?"

"I'm fine," Tamaya said, trying her best to sound normal.

"Mushroom, peppers, and onions okay?"

"No onions."

"I'll tell them to just put the onions on my half."

Tamaya didn't argue, even though she knew her half would still taste oniony.

"I'll be home as soon as I can. Love you."

"Love you too," Tamaya said. She waited until she heard the click on the other end, then hung up.

She finished with the Band-Aid, then returned to her bedroom, where she changed out of her dirty clothes and into flannel pajamas. There was no reason that should make her mother suspicious, she thought. Now that the nights were colder, she and her mother both liked getting into their soft and cozy pajamas, although usually *after* dinner. They'd drink hot apple cider and either watch TV together or, more often lately, work side by side.

She gathered up her dirty clothes and took them to the laundry nook.

There was nothing suspicious about her doing her own laundry either. She'd been doing it ever since she'd needed her favorite purple top for Monica's birthday party last year. Once when Marshall and his mother had been at her house, Tamaya's mother had said, "I suppose if Tamaya waited around for me to wash her clothes, she'd have to go to school naked."

Tamaya had been so embarrassed and so mortified by what her mother had said, *in front of Marshall,* that she'd run to her room and hadn't come out until after Marshall and his mother had left. Even now, she blushed thinking about it.

She dumped her dirty clothes into the washing machine, added soap, set the temperature, and then started it up. Listening to the swish of the water, she imagined she felt something like the way a murderer felt after he successfully destroyed all the evidence.

Her right hand was still tingling like crazy. She went into her mother's bathroom and searched the drawers and cabinets, not sure what she was searching for. She came across a blue jar of something called "restorative hand cream." The label said it was for dry, cracked, and irritated skin.

Tamaya removed the lid and dipped her fingers into the white, chalky ointment. She smeared it all over the bumpy spots. It felt cool and soothing. It seemed to work almost immediately. The bumps didn't look as red, and the tingling wasn't as bad.

From the other side of the wall, she could hear the rattle and buzz of the garage door opening. Her mother was home.

$$2 \times 4 = 8$$
$$2 \times 8 = 16$$

Her mother set down the pizza, kissed Tamaya on the cheek, and said, "Help yourself. I just need to answer this one email."

The pizza box smelled of onions. Tamaya had to pick off a few strays before putting a slice on her plate. She had to do it all left-handed, so as not to get any of the restorative hand cream on her food.

One email turned into six, but that was fine with Tamaya. The more her mother was wrapped up in work, the fewer questions Tamaya would have to answer.

Her mother had made a salad as she'd read through her emails. She rarely did only one thing at a time.

"So, did Ms. Filbert like your report?" she asked as she set the salad on the table.

"We ran out of time," Tamaya told her. "She didn't get to mine."

"That's too bad," her mother said. "You worked so hard on it."

Her mother's hair and eyes were dark like Tamaya's, but she had lighter skin. She liked colorful clothes. Her green eye shadow matched her blouse.

Tamaya shrugged. "I'll do it tomorrow. No one cares about Calvin Coolidge anyway."

Tamaya would have preferred to give her report on a different president, but by the time Ms. Filbert had gotten around to calling on her, all the good presidents had already been taken.

That was typical. Tamaya had sat quietly with her hand

raised, but then someone else had shouted out, "I want Lincoln," and then someone else had claimed Washington. Ms. Filbert had assigned those presidents to the shouters, even though she had just told the class, "Sit quietly and wait until I call on you."

It was Ms. Filbert who had suggested Calvin Coolidge to Tamaya when it had finally been her turn. "He was a lot like you, Tamaya," she had said. "They called him Silent Cal because he was known for being quiet."

Ms. Filbert had said "being quiet" as though it were some sort of abnormal behavior. *You're the one who just told everyone to sit quietly,* Tamaya had thought.

After dinner, Tamaya and her mother were working side by side on the living room sofa. The TV was on, but they were hardly watching. Her mother had a computer on her lap, and Tamaya's notebook paper was on the coffee table next to her history book.

She wasn't supposed to just look things up on the Internet. Tablets and smart phones were prohibited at Woodridge Academy. The headmistress, Mrs. Thaxton, wanted the students to do it the old-fashioned way. Even calculators were off-limits.

Tamaya's mother looked up from her laptop and asked if Tamaya had washed her hands after dinner. "You have pizza sauce on you."

Tamaya looked at her hand. It wasn't pizza sauce. Despite her mother's hand cream, the red bumps had returned. They had gotten bigger, and there seemed to be more of them. The tingling sensation had also returned, although she hadn't noticed it so much until now.

She couldn't keep it from her mother any longer. "It's not pizza," she said. "I think I might have some kind of rash."

She held out her hand.

Tamaya and her mother each had the same habit of biting their lower lip when thinking hard. Her mother was biting it now as she examined Tamaya's rash.

"It feels all funny too," Tamaya told her.

"Do you know how you got it?"

"I noticed it after school" was all she could say. She had promised Marshall not to tell her mother or anyone else about the woods. "I put some of your stuff on it."

"What stuff?"

"Restorative hand cream? In a blue jar?"

"Good," her mother said. "I use it all the time. It absolutely works miracles."

Tamaya was glad to hear that.

"I've got a meeting tomorrow morning," her mother told her, "but if you want, I can cancel and take you to see Dr. Sanchez."

"No, it's not that bad," Tamaya said. "I'll put more of the hand cream on it before I go to bed."

"We'll see how it looks in the morning," her mother said.

Later, Tamaya thought that maybe she should have agreed to let her mother take her to see Dr. Sanchez. At least she wouldn't have had to worry about Chad ambushing her on the way to school.

"You're next, Tamaya."

Still, would a seventh-grade boy really beat up a fifth-grade girl at school, with teachers all around? She doubted it. He might just push her down or something, but then she could blame her torn sweater on him. Then Chad's parents would have to buy her a new one. In a way it was sort of true. If it weren't for Chad, her sweater wouldn't have a hole in it.

Once again, she examined the hole in her sweater. She had tried looping some of the threads back through the hole and decided that maybe it wasn't all that noticeable.

Tamaya had another reason for not wanting to go to the doctor in the morning. It was something she'd never admit to her friends.

She had never missed a day of school. At the end of each school year, she'd been presented with a certificate for perfect attendance. Those certificates didn't mean quite as much to her now as they had when she'd been in the second and third grade, but still, she hated to spoil her perfect record.

Before going to bed, she said her prayers, and on this night, she included Chad Hilligas. She didn't pray for anything bad to happen to him. She asked God to help Chad find the goodness that lived inside his heart.

$$2 \times 16 = 32$$
$$2 \times 32 = 64$$

10

Tamaya slept. Marshall did not. As much as Chad had tormented him, he tormented himself even more.

He lay in bed, desperate to fall sleep. He knew he'd have to be alert to deal with Chad, but sleep seldom comes to those who are desperate for it. It is something that has to be eased into gently.

He'd gotten in trouble for coming home so late from school. He was supposed to have looked after the twins, and when he hadn't shown, his dad had had to leave work early.

"The only way we can afford to keep you at Woodridge is for everyone to do their part," his father had reminded him.

"Good. I'll go to another school, then," Marshall had answered. "I hate that place."

It didn't make any sense to Marshall. If his parents couldn't afford it, and he hated it, then why not let him go to another school? But that argument only made his parents angrier. Then, on his way back to his room, he'd accidentally stomped on the twins' hippo village, which had just caused more yelling.

"You're lucky I didn't step on you!" he'd told Daniela.

The whole thing was his parents' fault, Marshall decided. His birthday was September 29, and back when he was four years old, his parents had had to make a choice: either he could start kindergarten as one of the youngest kids in the class or he could wait a year and be one of the oldest. If they had waited, he'd be older, bigger, and stronger, and Chad Hilligas wouldn't even be in the same grade.

"How many members are in the U.S. Senate?" That was the question Mr. Davison had asked Chad.

"Twenty-nine?" Chad had guessed.

Andy was the one who had laughed, not Marshall. "How can there only be twenty-nine senators?" Andy had pointed out. "There are fifty states!"

But then Mr. Davison had said, "Marshall, will you kindly tell Chad how many senators there are?"

Right then, Marshall had known he was doomed. He had considered giving a wrong answer, and maybe he should have, but who knows? If he'd said something like "twenty-eight" or "a million," Chad might have thought Marshall was mocking him.

Instead, what Marshall had done was stare down at his desk and very quietly say, "One hundred, I guess."

It was only a short time later that Chad had nearly thrown him down the stairs. "We need to settle this once and for all. And you better be there, you thumb-sucking coward!"

Now, as he lay wide-awake at two-thirty in the morning, Marshall tried to convince himself that since Chad had finally beaten him up, he wouldn't bother him anymore. They had settled it *once and for all*.

Except he knew the opposite was more likely. Now that Chad had tasted blood, he would come back for more. And he would come after Tamaya too.

He imagined walking to school with her. She's yammering away about Monica or Calvin Coolidge or something, when Chad grabs her hair, spins her around, and punches her in the face!

"Leave her alone!" Marshall shouts.

Tamaya is on the ground, crying. Chad is about to hit Tamaya again, but Marshall grabs his arm. "I said, leave her alone, Buttface!"

Chad shoves him. He shoves Chad back. A crowd gathers.

Chad comes at him with all he's got, punching wildly, but Marshall holds his ground, ducking and hitting back.

At first, Marshall hears everyone rooting for Chad, but as the fight continues, he starts to hear a few of his old friends root for him. *"Get 'im, Marshall!" "You can do it, Marshall!"*

And then . . .

As Marshall tried to fall asleep, he imagined the fight ending in different ways. Sometimes he was the winner, leaving Chad beaten and bloody, begging for mercy. Other times, Chad won, but only after a long, hard-fought battle.

He envisioned himself lying on the pavement, barely able to move. Two pretty girls from his class, Andrea Gall and Laura Musscrantz, kneel by his side and tell him how brave he was as they dab the blood off his face with wet paper towels. Laura kisses his cheek.

But even as he imagined all this, he knew it would never happen.

If Chad attacked Tamaya, the best he could hope for was that a teacher would break it up before Tamaya got hurt too badly. Then maybe Chad would be expelled, and then maybe after Chad was gone for a while, the other kids would like him again.

That was his best hope, and he hated himself for it, because he knew it was the pathetic hope of a coward.

11

Poof!

Excerpted from the Senate's secret hearings:

> **SENATOR HALTINGS:** Of course, we all have great hope for a non-polluting, inexpensive alternative to gasoline. But my big concern, Mr. Fitzman, is what will happen when your man-made ergonyms mix with the natural environment. How will they affect plant and animal life? And ultimately human life? We just don't know.
>
> **JONATHAN FITZMAN:** I've got that covered.
>
> **SENATOR HALTINGS:** The smaller something is, the harder it is to keep it contained. You can put a tiger or a grizzly bear inside

a cage, but it's a lot harder to keep a tiny microorganism from escaping.

Jonathan Fitzman: Not a problem.

Senator Haltings: If you have your way, people will be filling their cars with Biolene at every gas station from Miami to Seattle. Tanker trucks will be hauling Biolene across the country. Drops will spill. Accidents will happen. Then what?

Jonathan Fitzman: Look, you got it all upside down and backward. You're all worried about ergonyms getting out, but really, it's just the opposite. I'm doing all I can to keep the outside from getting in.

Senator Haltings: I'm not sure I see the difference.

Jonathan Fitzman: Ergonyms can't survive in oxygen. Expose an ergie to oxygen, and poof!

Senator Haltings: Poof?

Jonathan Fitzman: It disintegrates. Poof. You don't have to worry about ergies escaping into the air. At SunRay Farm, we had to build special vacuum-sealed hoses and tanks, just to keep the air out.

12

Tamaya awoke to her favorite song. Cold air came through her window, purposely left open just a crack, making the warmth of the covers that much cozier.

Her music came on at 7:08 every morning, because eight was her favorite number, and Monica's favorite number was seven. Her best friend, Monica, also woke up each day at that exact time.

Tamaya's thoughts drifted back to last year. There was a huge fireplace in the back of her fourth-grade classroom. Her teacher had filled it with pillows, and when the students finished their work, they were allowed to go into the fireplace and read. The fireplace was so big, there was room in there for at least four kids, and she and Monica were usually the first two back there, side by side, reading their books and trying not to giggle.

As Tamaya was thinking about this, a growing sense of dread slowly crept into her memories. The image of the pillowed fireplace gave way to the woods, her torn sweater, and Chad. His cold eyes staring at her as he said, "You're next, Tamaya."

Her hand tingled. She brought it out from under her covers to have a look. At first she thought the rash had cleared, but as her eyes adjusted to the light, she realized the red bumps were still there, covered in some kind of powdery crust.

There was powder on her pillow too, and when she pulled back the sheets, she could see it all over the bed. It was a pinkish-bronze color, the same color as her skin.

She leapt out of bed and hurried to the bathroom.

The powder washed right off, but the rash had spread. Red bumps coated her entire hand and continued down to her wrist. Some of the bumps had turned into blisters.

Looking at herself in the mirror, she could see a crusty area on the right side of her face. She splashed it with water, and then scrubbed the entire area very hard with a soapy washcloth and very hot water.

There didn't appear to be any bumps on her face. It looked a little red, but that could have been from her scrubbing so hard.

Her mother's jar of miracle hand cream was in Tamaya's bathroom. The night before, she had dabbed a little bit on each bump and then gently rubbed it in. Now she went whole hog! She dug her fingers deep into the chalky ointment and pulled out a big glob of the stuff. She smeared it on thickly over the entire area.

She returned to her bedroom, where she bundled up her sheets. Then she took them to the washing machine. She set the temperature gauge to hot.

"You're washing your sheets *now*?"

Tamaya spun around.

Her mother was already dressed, wearing a cranberry-colored skirt and jacket. Her eye shadow was the same color as her clothes.

"Because of my rash," Tamaya told her. "So it doesn't spread."

"Let me see."

Tamaya held out her hand.

"It looks a little better, I think," her mother said.

Tamaya knew that was because it was covered up by the hand cream, but she didn't say anything. Her mother's breath smelled like toothpaste and coffee.

"Tell you what," her mother said. "You tell Marshall I'll be picking you up right after school today. I can give him a ride home too, if he wants, but then I'm taking you to see Dr. Sanchez."

Tamaya nodded, glad that her rash would get treated.

$$2 \times 64 = 128$$
$$2 \times 128 = 256$$

She put on her backpack, positioning the straps so they covered the hole in her sweater, then walked quickly through the house and on out the door before her mother could get too good a look at her. She still didn't know how she'd explain the hole.

She reached Marshall's house just as he was coming outside. He was wearing his old glasses.

He had switched from glasses to contacts over the summer. She liked his glasses better. She had thought his face looked blank without them.

"You're wearing your glasses," she said.

He shrugged, then said, "I lost my contacts in the woods."

"Oh."

In her mind she could see Chad slugging him in the face, his contacts flying out of his eyes, although she realized it might not have happened that way at all.

She could see no bruises on his face. He just looked tired and washed out, like he hadn't slept for six days.

He dragged his feet as he walked. On other days, Tamaya had to struggle just to keep up with him, but as they continued slowly up the sidewalk, she began to worry that they might be late.

Her tingling sensation had become more of a prickling. It felt as if her hand were being stabbed by a thousand very tiny needles.

"Oh, my mom's picking me up after school," she told Marshall. "She's taking me to the doctor, 'cause I got a rash or something in the woods."

She showed him her hand, but he hardly glanced at it.

"You didn't tell her we went in there, did you?" Marshall asked.

"No."

"Because if you did, we'd both be in big—"

"I said I didn't tell her."

"Good."

"She can give you a ride home too, if you want."

"Yeah, whatever," Marshall said, but she knew he was glad for the ride, glad to be safe from Chad.

They turned onto Richmond Road. There was a lot of early-morning traffic, and once again Tamaya realized how much safer Marshall would have been if they had just walked home the usual way. She wouldn't have torn her sweater. He wouldn't have lost his contacts. And she probably wouldn't have gotten the rash either, she thought, although she wasn't really sure how she'd gotten that.

As they walked alongside the woods, that feeling of dread she'd had when she'd first woken up returned. It seemed to grow a little heavier with each step.

She couldn't pinpoint exactly what it was she was dreading. She didn't think she was all that afraid of Chad, as long as other people were around. It was something different. Something worse. It was as if she knew something terrible was about to happen, but it was so bad, her brain wouldn't allow her to think about it.

They reached Woodridge Lane. "This is where I was supposed to meet him," said Marshall.

There was an area of weeds and dirt between the sidewalk and the fence. Tamaya figured that Chad must have climbed the fence and gone into the woods when Marshall didn't show up.

"At least there would have been people around," Tamaya pointed out. "It was worse in the woods."

"Don't remind me." He kicked at the ground.

Tamaya felt sorry for him. She didn't like feeling that way. She liked it better when she used to look up to Marshall.

"Chad's just a big jerk," she said.

"I don't care about him," Marshall muttered.

"A big fat jerk!" she repeated, loud enough so that if Chad was hiding nearby, he would definitely hear her.

They turned onto Woodridge Lane. The woods were on both sides of them as they headed toward the school.

Tamaya quickened her pace. "We'd better hurry so we're not late," she said, but Marshall continued to lag behind.

She walked faster and faster, and then something inside her made her want to run. It wasn't just the fear of being tardy. She felt scared—although of what, she didn't know.

She was out of breath when she reached the line of cars backed up from the school. Only then did she stop running.

She heard someone call her name.

Merilee, Monica's little sister, was hanging halfway out the window of her mother's Mercedes, waving to her.

Tamaya waved back using her left hand. She tried to keep her right one hidden. She waited by the curb as Merilee, and then Monica, climbed out of the car.

"Where were you yesterday?" Monica asked. "I kept trying to call."

Tamaya wanted to tell Monica everything but didn't dare risk it. She knew Monica would tell Hope, and then it would be all over the school. "I don't know," she said. "In and out."

"You need to get a cell phone," Monica told her.

"They're not allowed at school," Tamaya reminded her.

"You can use it after school," said Monica.

"I was in and out too," said Merilee. "And then I went in again, and then I went back out."

Monica told her sister to shut up. "So, you'll never believe who I saw yesterday," she said to Tamaya.

"Mr. Beauchamps," said Merilee.

"Shut up. I'm telling her. Mr. Beauchamps. He was jogging, right in front of my house! He sees me and says, *'Bonjour, Mademoiselle Monique.'* I swear I almost lost it."

Mr. Beauchamps had been their French teacher since the second grade.

"You wouldn't think a bald guy would have such hairy legs," said Monica.

Tamaya forced herself to smile.

Marshall was relieved to see Tamaya safely enter the

60

building with her friend Monica and with no sign of Chad. He wasn't sure what he would have done if Chad had attacked her. He liked to think he would have tried to protect her, but he also knew he might not have.

He reached the front door. The seventh grade was located in the basement. It had been the servants' quarters, but everyone at school called it the dungeon.

It felt like a dungeon to Marshall. He trudged on down the stairs, doomed to whatever torture and misery awaited.

13

Disaster Warning

Excerpted from the secret Senate hearings:

PROFESSOR ALICE MAYFAIR: When I was born, in 1975, there were four billion people living in the world. That's a lot. A hundred years ago, there were less than two billion. But today as I speak to this committee, there are more than seven billion of us.

SENATOR FOOTE: What does this have to do with Biolene?

PROFESSOR ALICE MAYFAIR: More than three hundred thousand babies are born every single day. Day after day, after day. Every one of them will need food, water, and energy.

Senator Foote: Exactly why this country needs Biolene.

Senator Wright: Excuse me, Professor. It was my understanding you were going to testify about possible disasters that could result from the man-made organisms being introduced into the environment. It sounds to me like you are in favor of Biolene.

Professor Alice Mayfair: Oh, there will be disasters. Whether from Biolene or something else, who knows? By the year 2050, an additional two billion people will inhabit this planet. Nine billion!

Senator Foote: Which is why we need Biolene.

Professor Alice Mayfair: Unless we do something to control world population, nothing will help us, Senator. Not Biolene, not super-duper crops and fertilizers, not colonies on Mars.

Senator Wright: Let me get this straight. You want us to keep people from having too many babies, all over the world?

Professor Alice Mayfair: Yes.

Senator March: [*Laughs.*] I'm afraid that's just a bit beyond the scope of this committee.

14

Mondays, Wednesdays, and Fridays, the students in Ms. Filbert's class had to write in their journals. Sometimes she let them write about whatever they wanted, but more often she gave them a prompt.

Tamaya preferred the prompts. It was strange, but she found it harder to think of something to write when she could write about anything in the world.

Most everyone else always moaned and groaned when they heard the prompts. It didn't seem to matter what the prompts were. Some people just liked to complain.

Today Ms. Filbert wrote the prompt on the whiteboard, then said it aloud.

"How to blow up a balloon."

Along with the usual moans and groans, there were a lot of *Huh?*s and *What?*s. Hands were raised all around Tamaya.

"I don't get it." Jason spoke out without raising his hand. "You just stick it into your mouth and blow."

"Oh, you mean like this?" asked Ms. Filbert.

Tamaya watched, wide-eyed, as her teacher took a red balloon and placed the whole thing inside her mouth. Ms. Filbert took a big breath, then blew, spitting the balloon out onto the floor.

Everyone laughed, including Tamaya. She smiled at Hope, who sat next to her, then tried to catch Monica's eye on the other side of the room. Monica was looking back at her, sharing her amazement.

Ms. Filbert scratched her head, as if she were greatly confused. "That didn't work," she said.

"No, you don't put the whole balloon into your mouth," said Jason, again without raising his hand. "Just one end."

Ms. Filbert slapped herself on the forehead. "Well, why didn't you say that in the first place?"

She chose another balloon and this time put only one end into her mouth—the wrong end.

"No, the other end!" called Monica.

Ms. Filbert turned the balloon around.

"Now blow," said Monica.

Once again, Ms. Filbert spit the balloon onto the floor.

All around Tamaya, kids were shouting instructions,

trying to tell Ms. Filbert what she had done wrong. Others were repeating to their friends what they'd just seen, even though their friends had just seen it too.

Ms. Filbert held up two fingers and waited for everyone to quiet down.

"Don't tell me," she said. "*Write it*. Pretend that what you write is going to be read by someone who never, ever saw a balloon before in her whole life. And she's none too bright neither." Ms. Filbert knocked on the side of her head, as if testing to see if it were hollow.

Tamaya laughed. Her mind was already working on her how-to-blow-up-a-balloon instructions.

"So your instructions have to be clear and precise," Ms. Filbert continued. "Later, you can read them aloud, and we'll see how many balloons I manage to inflate."

The complainers were moaning and groaning again, but Tamaya was up for the challenge. She picked up her pencil, thought a moment, then wrote:

You start with a flat balloon. You want to fill it with air from your lungs.

The rest of the class was still buzzing about their teacher's spitting balloons.

From across the aisle, Hope tapped Tamaya on the shoulder. "What happened to your sweater?" she whispered.

Tamaya's heart sank. She'd hoped it wasn't so noticeable. "What do you mean?" she whispered back.

"It's all torn."

Tamaya shrugged. "Who cares?" she said, trying to prove she wasn't the Goody Two-shoes that Hope thought she was.

She returned to her journal, reread what she had written, and then added, *Look for the end with the hole.*

No, she didn't like that. A hole was the last thing you wanted in a balloon! For all she knew, Ms. Filbert might stick a pin into the balloon, just to put a hole there!

She tried to think of what else to call it. The knobby round thing?

She tried to erase what she had written but instead made an ugly gray smudge on her paper. Tamaya's pages were always clean and neat, and she had excellent handwriting. She tried rubbing harder but not hard enough to tear the page.

A red drop fell on top of the smudge.

At first, Tamaya was more worried about her journal being ruined than anything else. But when she looked at her hand, she was horrified to see it was covered with blisters and blood.

She dropped her pencil. It rolled across her journal, leaving a red track behind it, then continued across her desk and fell to the floor.

"Ms. Filbert!" called Hope. "Tamaya's all bloody!"

$$2 \times 256 = 512$$
$$2 \times 512 = 1{,}024$$

15

Down in the Dungeon

There was still no sign of Chad when Marshall walked into his classroom and took his seat. His relief quickly turned into anxiety, however. He turned his head toward the door every single time he heard it open. He knew Chad would come waltzing in at any moment, telling everyone about what had happened in the woods, and about how Marshall had needed a little fifth-grade girl to protect him.

Even after class started, and Chad still hadn't shown, Marshall's anxiety only grew worse. He tapped his foot throughout morning announcements. In a way, he hoped Chad would hurry up and get there. Let him do what he was going to do, say what he was going to say, and get it over with. The worst part was the waiting.

When first period ended, Marshall moved very cautiously through the hall, certain that Chad was waiting behind every corner. He made it safely to algebra, and when he saw that Chad's desk was empty, he finally was able to relax, but just a little bit.

Math had always been Marshall's best subject, and without Chad's eyes burning a hole through the back of his head, he was able to concentrate for the first time in weeks.

Mr. Brandt put a pair of simultaneous equations on the whiteboard. Marshall mentally went through the necessary steps to solve them just as his teacher worked them through for the class.

Mr. Brandt put up two more equations. "Anyone want to try?"

Chad or no Chad, Marshall still didn't dare raise his hand.

Perhaps Mr. Brandt had caught something in Marshall's expression, an alertness in his eyes. "Marshall," he said. "You want to give it a go?"

Marshall flinched at the mention of his name, then slowly rose. As he made his way to the front of the room, he heard none of the usual snide whispers. No legs stuck out trying to trip him.

He took the marker from Mr. Brandt, studied the two equations for a moment, and then wrote a new equation, combining elements from the other two. He felt his confidence grow as he replaced letters with numbers.

Behind him, the door opened.

It couldn't even have been called a squeak, just an old door rotating on its hinges, but Marshall recognized the sound the moment he heard it.

His confidence left him as his legs turned to jelly. He tried to concentrate on the equations in front of him, but now it was all just a confused jumble of numbers, letters, and mathematical signs.

He heard the click-click of hard shoes on the floor. That didn't sound like Chad. He slowly turned.

The headmistress, Mrs. Thaxton, was walking purposefully toward the front of the room, a stern and determined look on her face.

"I'm sorry to interrupt, Mr. Brandt," she said, then turned her back on Marshall in order to face the class. "I'm afraid I have some very disturbing news."

Marshall didn't know where he was supposed to go. He didn't want to have to cross in front of Mrs. Thaxton in order to return to his desk. Instead, he slowly edged away from the board, toward the side wall.

She spoke slowly and deliberately. "One of your classmates, Chad Hilligas, is missing. He hasn't been seen since he left school yesterday afternoon. As far as we know, he never made it home."

Mrs. Thaxton took a breath, then continued. "If any of you know anything about where he might have gone, or what has happened to him, I need to know immediately."

Nobody said a word.

As Marshall stood at the side wall, his thoughts were a

swirling mass of confusion. He had become paralyzed at the mention of Chad's name. He could hear the pounding of his heart echoing inside his head.

"Does anybody remember seeing Chad after school yesterday?" asked Mr. Brandt.

"If you saw or heard anything?" coaxed Mrs. Thaxton.

Marshall knew he ought to say something, but it seemed impossible.

Laura Musscrantz slowly raised her hand.

"Yes, Laura," said Mr. Brandt.

"I saw him."

"Where?"

"On Richmond Road."

"Did he say anything to you?" Mrs. Thaxton asked her.

"No, I was in my mom's car. We just drove past. You asked if we saw him. That's all."

Marshall wondered if Laura would have noticed him too, if he had been there.

"Did you notice which way he was heading?" asked Mrs. Thaxton.

"If you leave the school and turn right. I think. We drove the other way, so I didn't see him after that."

"Did anyone else see or talk to Chad?" asked Mrs. Thaxton. "Either after school or perhaps earlier? Did he say what his plans were for after school?"

Cody raised his hand, then quickly lowered it, but not before Mr. Brandt noticed. "Do you know something, Cody?"

"He kind of told me what he was going to do, but I feel weird saying it."

"What did he tell you, Cody?" demanded Mrs. Thaxton. "This is not the time to worry about being embarrassed or *feeling weird*."

"Okay, you asked." Cody shrugged. "He said he was going to beat up Marshall."

Muffled laughter came from the back corner of the room, but one look from Mrs. Thaxton silenced whoever had laughed.

"Sorry, man," Cody said, looking at Marshall. "That's what he said."

For the first time, Mrs. Thaxton turned to notice Marshall, standing awkwardly against the wall. "Marshall, what do you know about this?"

All he could manage was a shrug. It took all his effort just to keep from trembling.

"Did you encounter Chad on your way home yesterday?"

He shook his head.

"Did you know he was looking for you?"

"No," he said.

"You didn't see him at all?"

"I just walked home like always. He wasn't there."

Mrs. Thaxton took a long hard look at him. "Do you know why he wanted to fight you? Did something happen earlier?"

He shook his head.

"Chad's been picking on Marshall all year," said Andy. "For no reason."

"Marshall never did anything," volunteered Laura. "Chad's just mean."

Mrs. Thaxton took another long look at Marshall, then turned her attention back to the rest of the class. "If anybody thinks of anything else, any little thing Chad might have done or said, or something somebody else might have said about Chad, please let Mr. Brandt or me know. If you need to talk in private, I will be in my office. Please think hard, and don't be afraid to come to me. I will keep anything you tell me strictly confidential."

She walked out of the room. Then all eyes fixed on Marshall.

He quickly returned to his seat. The equations remained on the whiteboard, unsolved.

16

Using cotton balls and hydrogen peroxide, Mrs. Latherly cleaned the blood off Tamaya's hand. "You mustn't scratch it," she admonished.

"I didn't," said Tamaya.

"The more you scratch, the worse it will get," said Mrs. Latherly. "It will just cause the rash to spread. Plus, anytime you break the skin, there's the possibility of infection."

"I didn't scratch it," Tamaya repeated.

She was seated in a plastic chair in an alcove inside the office. The alcove contained the office printer and the coffee-maker. The medical supplies were on a shelf next to the printer.

Mrs. Latherly spent most days answering phones or working on a computer, but whenever anyone got sick or needed first aid, she was the person to see.

"Maybe I rubbed it a little," Tamaya admitted. "But it doesn't itch. It feels tingly. You know how like when your hands are really cold, and then you stick them under warm water? The way they get all prickly. That's how it feels."

"Uh-huh," Mrs. Latherly said as she took a first-aid box off the shelf, but Tamaya didn't think she was really listening.

She watched Mrs. Latherly unlatch the lid, then take out various tubes, read the labels, and put them back. Tamaya really wished Mrs. Latherly would hurry. She still hoped she could get back to class in time to finish her journal entry.

In her mind, she imagined Hope and Jason and Monica taking turns reading their how-to-blow-up-a-balloon instructions to Ms. Filbert. She could see the balloons flying out of her teacher's mouth and jetting in circles around the room while everyone laughed.

It isn't fair, she thought. *Why do I always have to miss out on all the fun stuff?*

It seemed to be that way all the time. She'd missed Hope's limousine birthday party because it had been her weekend to be in Philadelphia. And then Katie, her only sort-of friend in Philadelphia, had invited her to go horseback riding in the country with her and her family, but that too had been for the wrong weekend.

Mr. Franks, the assistant headmaster, stepped into the

alcove. "Hi, Tamaya," he greeted her. "You're not sick, are you?"

"No, just a rash."

"Good. We don't want to ruin your perfect record." He winked at her.

Tamaya could feel her face get warm, and she tried very hard not to blush. All her friends agreed that Mr. Franks was movie-star handsome. Summer swore he had a tattoo on the back of his neck, which was why he always wore a jacket and tie. Summer didn't know what the tattoo was, but it was definitely something *inappropriate*. If Mrs. Thaxton found out about it, he would be fired.

Mr. Franks bent down to pour himself a cup of coffee, and Tamaya tried to get a peek at his neck. She couldn't see anything. She doubted he really had a tattoo. After all, how could Summer know about it, and not Mrs. Thaxton?

"Hold out your hand," said Mrs. Latherly.

Tamaya waited for Mr. Franks to leave the alcove. She didn't want him to see her ugly rash. "I tried some of my mother's hand cream," she told Mrs. Latherly. "It didn't work."

"This will," Mrs. Latherly assured her.

As Mrs. Latherly applied the ointment, Tamaya read the label on the upside-down tube. *Hydrocortisone 1%*. She took heart in the words *Maximum Strength*.

"Do you have any pets?" Mrs. Latherly asked.

"Cooper, my dog."

"Do you think you might be allergic to Cooper?"

"No!" she exclaimed. That would be horrible. Cooper was the best part of going to her dad's. He slept on the same bed with her, and she often woke up with the dog licking her face.

"Has Cooper had any kind of problems lately, with fleas or ticks or mange?"

"I hope not," said Tamaya.

Mrs. Latherly looked confused. "Has he or hasn't he?"

Tamaya explained that she saw Cooper only one weekend a month.

Mrs. Latherly seemed exasperated. "Tamaya, I'm trying to determine what might have caused your rash. If you haven't been near Cooper, then it obviously didn't come from him."

"Sorry," Tamaya said. She felt stupid.

It felt confusing sometimes, having two different homes. It was like she had two different lives; two half lives. And the two added together didn't quite equal a whole life. She felt like she was missing something.

Mrs. Latherly wrapped Tamaya's hand with gauze. "Is there anything else you might have touched recently that you can think of?" she asked. "Maybe some kind of cleaning product?"

Tamaya wondered if she should tell Mrs. Latherly about the strange mud. She didn't want to get Marshall in trouble. Still, she knew it was important to tell the truth to a doctor or nurse, even if Mrs. Latherly was just a part-time school nurse.

"Well, there was this fuzzy mud," she admitted.

"Have you eaten peanuts or peanut butter?" asked Mrs. Latherly, showing no interest in the mud.

Tamaya's mind remained fixed on the fuzzy mud. It all had happened so quickly, but replaying it in her head, in slow motion, she could see herself picking up a handful of the tar-like muck. She vaguely recalled that it had felt warm, although she couldn't be certain that she wasn't just embellishing her memory.

"Have you recently eaten any peanuts or peanut butter?" Mrs. Latherly asked again.

Tamaya forced herself to focus on the question. "I had a peanut butter and jelly sandwich yesterday," she said. "It might have been the day before."

"You may be allergic," said Mrs. Latherly. "Next time you see your doctor, have your mother ask for an allergy test. In the meantime, I wouldn't eat any more peanut butter sandwiches."

"My mom makes her own strawberry jam," Tamaya offered up. "Out of real strawberries. Maybe I'm allergic to that."

"Maybe," said Mrs. Latherly.

"She's taking me to the doctor after school."

"Good."

Mrs. Latherly wrapped each of Tamaya's fingers separately, then her palm and wrist.

"How does that feel?"

Tamaya tried to wiggle her fingers. "Like I'm a mummy," she joked.

Mrs. Latherly smiled. "I'd like to give you an allergy pill too, but I need to get your mother's permission. I'll call her at work. Check back with me after lunch."

Tamaya said she would.

"And remember, no more scratching!"

$$2 \times 1{,}024 = 2{,}048$$
$$2 \times 2{,}048 = 4{,}096$$

17

By the time Tamaya made it back to Ms. Filbert's, the class had already moved on to math. There were two inflated balloons taped to the bulletin board. She learned later that only Sam and Rashona had succeeded with their how-to-blow-up-a-balloon instructions. And, according to Hope, Ms. Filbert had had to fudge just a little bit to get those to work.

Throughout the morning, Tamaya felt a pang of disappointment every time she glanced up at the two balloons. She was sure she could have had a balloon up there too, and with no fudging.

She had to write left-handed, which was nearly impossible. Even if it was math, she had a terrible time just trying to make the number two.

"So what's wrong with your hand?" Hope asked her.

"I'm not supposed to eat peanut butter," she whispered.

"Peanut butter makes your hand bleed?"

She shrugged. She didn't want to talk about it. Not with Hope. But she didn't think her rash had anything to do with peanuts or peanut butter.

It had to be the fuzzy mud.

$$2 \times 4{,}096 = 8{,}192$$
$$2 \times 8{,}192 = 16{,}384$$

Plastic bags were no longer allowed at Woodridge Academy, and no one past the second grade would be caught dead holding a lunch box. Tamaya and her friends carried their lunches in reusable cloth sacks.

Monica's sack was black with a rhinestone peace sign. Hope's was also black, with a red heart. Tamaya's was plain white, frayed around the edges from its many trips through the washer and dryer.

The girls headed down the stairs toward the lunchroom. "If they ask you about why your hand is all bandaged," Hope said, "don't tell them it's a rash."

Tamaya didn't know who "they" were. She figured Hope was just talking about the other kids in the lunchroom.

"Rashes are gross," Monica agreed.

"Tell them you stabbed yourself with a pencil!" said Hope.

"That's gross too," Tamaya pointed out.

"But it's the kind of gross that boys like," said Monica.

Tamaya still didn't know what they were talking about.

Summer, who was in the other fifth-grade class, was waiting for them just outside the lunchroom. "What happened to you?" she asked when she saw Tamaya.

"She stabbed herself with a pencil," Monica answered, before Tamaya could say anything.

Summer looked very worried. "Why?"

"Just because," said Hope.

"Not really," Tamaya whispered.

The four girls entered the lunchroom. "Act like you don't know they're there," Monica said as she set out toward the same table where they had sat the day before. The older boys were already there. The lunch period for the upper grades began fourteen minutes before that for the middle grades.

Tamaya was relieved not to see Chad with the group of boys, although she was curious where he was. Looking around, she didn't see Marshall either. She hoped nothing bad had happened.

"Don't look at them!" Monica sharply whispered.

"We're just sitting where we always sit," said Summer.

"If they happen to be there too," said Hope, "well, that's just a coincidence."

Tamaya bit her lip. She wondered when her friends had decided that they'd sit next to the boys again. Or maybe they hadn't talked about it. Maybe it was one of those things she was *just supposed to know*.

The girls stepped over the benches and sat down at the table without even glancing at the boys. Tamaya kept her eyes down.

"What happened to her?" asked one of the boys.

Summer turned. "Oh, hi," she said, as if just noticing the boys were there.

"Tamaya stabbed herself with her pencil," said Monica. She smiled at the boy.

"It went right through her hand," said Hope. "In one side and out the other!"

"Cool."

Tamaya examined the contents of her lunch and didn't look up. She knew they were all staring at her. If she could have, she would have crawled inside her sack.

"Didn't it hurt?" asked the boy next to her.

Tamaya's heart was beating very fast as she continued to concentrate on her lunch. She had a sandwich, a juice box, a granola bar, and a container of sliced fruit.

"Course it hurt," said Summer. "What do you think?"

The boy touched Tamaya's other arm, just above the elbow. "Why?" he asked.

It took all her courage to turn and look at him.

"Why not?" she replied.

The boy continued to stare. He was obviously very impressed.

She smiled.

At least nobody thought she was a Goody Two-shoes anymore.

"So, did you guys hear about Chad?" asked one of the other boys.

Tamaya felt as though she'd been jolted by a thousand volts of electricity. "What about Chad?" she asked.

"He's gone," said the boy next to her.

"He's been missing since yesterday afternoon," said another. "He never made it home."

All the boys were talking at once.

"The police are looking for him."

"He's probably in jail somewhere."

"He'd already stolen, like, ten cars."

Tamaya's head was spinning. Again, she looked around the lunchroom for Marshall.

"If he was in jail, then wouldn't the police know where he was?" asked Hope.

"Not if he didn't tell them his name."

Tamaya's feeling of dread returned, stronger than ever. It wasn't her rash, or her ruined sweater, or having to lie to her mother, or the fear of being beaten up by Chad. It was worse than all of that.

It was this.

She stood up. Then a rush of dizziness made her grab the edge of the table.

"Are you all right?" asked Summer.

Taking her lunch, she nearly fell over the bench as she stepped away from the table. She had to find Marshall!

"Where are you going?" asked Monica.

As she moved through the lunchroom, desperately looking for Marshall, she could hear different groups of kids talking about Chad.

"He climbed up on top of the school and is trapped up there and can't get down."

"He joined a motorcycle gang and is on his way to Mexico."

"He got into a knife fight and is lying in some hospital with amnesia. He can't even remember his name."

Everybody seemed to think that whatever had happened to Chad, it had to be his own fault. He was a bad kid, and bad kids do bad things, and then bad things happen to them.

Nobody suspected that it was a good kid who was really to blame. *A Goody Two-shoes with perfect attendance who had done only one bad thing in her whole entire life!*

Tamaya went down the hall and pushed open the door. She felt a welcome blast of cold air. She took a deep breath as she looked out past the soccer field to the woods.

Chad was out there somewhere. She was sure of it.

How else could she and Marshall have gotten away from him so easily? It was because she had smashed the glob of fuzzy mud into his face. Deep down, she must have known it all along.

She looked at her bandages, covering not only her rash but

also her guilt. Whatever was happening to her hand, Chad's face had to be ten times worse.

She spotted Marshall. He was playing basketball with a group of boys. She had never been so relieved to see anyone.

"Marshall!" she shouted, then ran toward the game, calling his name two more times.

He glanced at her as she neared the court, but then kept on playing.

"I have to talk to you!"

He ignored her.

Boys were running up the court. The basketball flew through the air and bounced off the rim, and then the boys were running the other way.

"Oh, come on!" she exclaimed.

She knew he didn't want her talking to him at school, but that didn't even make sense anymore. For the last two days she'd been eating lunch with other older boys. If they weren't embarrassed to be seen with her, why should he be? It wasn't like anyone would accuse him of having "cooties."

"It's important!" she yelled to him.

Someone threw him the ball. He caught it, took a quick look at her, and then dribbled twice and passed it to someone else.

The boys were all down to their shirts. She stepped over their crumpled blue sweaters as she moved up and down the sideline, staying even with Marshall, trying to catch his eye. He wouldn't look at her.

She studied her bandaged hand and thought, *Maybe I really do have cooties.*

The ball clanked off the edge of the backboard and was coming her way. She raced after it and caught it on the third bounce.

A boy came toward her, hands out, expectantly.

"I have to talk to Marshall," she said.

"C'mon, girl. Just give me the ball," said the boy.

Tamaya held the ball against her chest, wrapping her arms around it.

"What's your problem, girl?" he demanded.

Marshall came toward her. "Quit being a pest," he said.

"Chad's missing," she told him. Although, as she said it aloud, she realized he must have known that already.

"So?" he asked.

He put his hands on the ball. She held tight for a moment, then loosened her grip and let him take it.

She waited by the court for the game to end, her eyes constantly returning to the woods. The lunch period for the upper grades ended fourteen minutes before the one for the middle grades. When the bell finally rang, she hung back as the boys were retrieving their sweaters, then slowly approached Marshall.

"What?" he snapped.

"We were the last to see him," she said. "We have to tell someone."

The other boys were heading back to the building.

"No, Tamaya," Marshall said firmly. "You can't tell anyone, ever. Look, he's the one who hit me. I didn't hit him. Besides, it's got nothing to do with us, anyway. He ran away from home or something."

She held up her bandaged hand. "Look at my hand!"

"I know, you told me. Your mom's taking you to the doctor."

"Look at it!" she screamed as she pulled at the bandages and ripped away the medical tape.

As the gauze pulled loose, a powdery substance sprinkled out, the same powder that had been in her bed earlier.

Marshall stared. Even Tamaya was stunned by how much worse her rash had gotten, just since Mrs. Latherly had treated it. Huge blisters, bleeding and crusted over, now covered the entire area, from the tip of her fingers down past her wrist. Smaller bumps extended halfway to her elbow.

"That's . . . really bad," said Marshall.

"The mud in the woods," Tamaya said. "I think it's dangerous. I picked it up with this hand, and then smashed it into Chad's face."

She was afraid she was about to cry, but fought it off. *"Into his face!"* she screamed.

"So?"

"Why do you think he didn't chase after us? He's still out there, and it's *all my fault*!"

"You don't know that for sure," said Marshall.

"I have to tell Mrs. Thaxton."

"No, you can't!" Marshall insisted. "I already told her that I didn't see Chad yesterday. What are you going to say? We walked home together, and you saw him but I didn't? Think about it, Tamaya. 'Oh, now I remember, Mrs. Thaxton. I did see Chad yesterday. He beat me up in the woods. I just forgot.'"

"I have to tell somebody."

"It's just mud. And anyway, I heard he joined a motorcycle gang and is on his way to Mexico."

"You *know* that's not true," said Tamaya.

"I don't *know* anything," said Marshall. "And neither do you."

He turned away from her. She stared after him as he headed to the building. He never looked back once.

Fourteen minutes later, Tamaya was still out by the basketball court when the bell rang for her to go in. She didn't know what to do. She didn't want to get Marshall in trouble, but *somebody had to do something!* She remained there, motionless, as kids all around her returned to the building.

Once again, she gazed out into the woods. She took a step toward the soccer field. Then another.

She walked slowly at first, but her pace increased with every step. She tried not to think about Ms. Filbert or Mrs. Thaxton. She started to run.

Her lunch sack swung from her hand. She was glad she still had it. Chad must be hungry.

$$2 \times 16,384 = 32,768$$
$$2 \times 32,768 = 65,536$$

18

It had been more than a month since Marshall had played basketball with his friends. A month since he'd had any friends, and all it had taken was a day—*just one day*—without Chad.

"Marshall never did anything," Laura Musscrantz had said. "Chad's just mean!"

Those may have been the sweetest words he'd ever heard in his whole life.

Still, as he sat at his desk in Mr. Davison's class, three seats away from Chad's empty desk, he couldn't get the image of Tamaya's grotesque hand out of his mind; torn strips of bloody gauze had dangled from her blistered flesh. He saw her eyes too. They pleaded with him to do the right thing.

Man, just when things are finally going good for me, he thought. *Why do girls always have to go and ruin everything?*

He knew the right thing to do. He had known it when Mrs. Thaxton had come into his classroom and told everyone that Chad was missing.

The only reason he hadn't told her the truth right then and there was because he didn't want to get Tamaya in trouble. That was what he told himself. He had kept quiet for Tamaya's sake.

But deep down, he knew that was not the truth. He had remained silent because he was scared. Scared and ashamed.

Not that it mattered anymore. He knew it was just a matter of time before Tamaya told someone, either her teacher, Ms. Filbert, or else Mrs. Thaxton.

The classroom phone buzzed, and the sound seemed to vibrate deep down into his bones. As he watched Mr. Davison speak into the phone, he tried to read the expression on his teacher's face. His leg trembled beneath his desk.

Mr. Davison hung up, and Marshall quickly cast his eyes downward, pretending to concentrate on his open book.

"Marshall, Mrs. Thaxton would like to see you in her office."

He'd been expecting that, but the words still came as a jolt. His chair squeaked as he pushed back from his desk. He stood up, and then walked out of the room, desperately trying to appear calm.

He started up the stairs. Nothing made sense anymore.

Chad beat him up, yet he was the one who was getting in trouble!

Everyone was so worried about *poor Chad.* "Where's Chad?" "Did you see him?" "Did you talk to him?" "What did he say?"

Chad's missing? Good! He's gone, and I'm glad he's gone!

Did that make him a bad person?

He reached the top of the stairs. The office was to the right, but Marshall's eyes were drawn the other way, down a short hallway to a door with a window. Daylight shone through the window.

He stared at the door for a long moment. Maybe it was time people started worrying about *poor Marshall,* he thought.

He stared a moment longer, but then turned and headed toward the office. Tamaya was right. It was time to tell the truth.

Mrs. Latherly had her back to him and was bent over as she placed a folder in a filing cabinet.

"Mrs. Thaxton asked to see me," he said.

The school secretary straightened up. "Oh, hi, Marshall. We're glad you're here."

He wondered what she meant by that. She sent him on back to Mrs. Thaxton's office.

The headmistress's door was open. He could see her sitting at her desk, staring out the window.

He stepped inside and cleared his throat. "You wanted to see me?"

She turned. "Do you know where Tamaya is?"

It wasn't the question he'd expected, and for a moment he wondered if it was some kind of trick.

Mrs. Thaxton's face quivered. "Do you?" she demanded.

"Ms. Filbert's class?"

"She's not there. She never returned after lunch. I know you two spend a lot of time together."

"Not a lot. We walk to school together. You know, because we live on the same street. Her mom won't let her walk to school alone."

The words were coming out of his mouth as his mind was busily trying to come to grips with what was happening. "Monica's her best friend," he said. "Maybe she knows."

"I spoke to Monica. She said Tamaya suddenly left the lunchroom, for no reason, and never came back. Where were you at lunch?"

"Outside, playing basketball."

"Did you see her?"

"Um, let me think. I think I might have seen her by the court."

"Did she say anything to you?"

"Now I remember. The ball bounced away, and she got it, and I went and got it from her."

"She didn't say anything about leaving school early?"

"Well, this morning she told me her mom was picking her up after school to take her to see a doctor. She's got this really bad rash. Maybe her mom picked her up early?"

"Mrs. Latherly left a message for her mother. We're waiting to hear back."

"Tamaya's pretty good about following rules," Marshall pointed out. "She wouldn't just leave without telling someone."

"I know," said Mrs. Thaxton. "That's exactly what worries me."

Marshall waited, but for a long time Mrs. Thaxton didn't say anything. She was looking at him, but it felt more like she was looking *through* him, as if she had forgotten he was still there.

"You can go now," she said at last.

He didn't have to be told twice.

A short while later, Mrs. Thaxton announced over the PA system that the school was being put on lockdown. Students and teachers were to remain in their classes with the lights off and the doors locked. No one would be allowed to enter or leave the building.

But by then, Marshall had already slipped out the side door. Like an escaping prisoner, he had dashed across the grass, frantically climbed over the fence, and then disappeared into the woods.

19

WEDNESDAY, NOVEMBER 3
1:10 P.M.

Leaves continued to fall around Tamaya as she wandered through the trees, hoping to see something, *anything,* that looked familiar from the day before. Then, at least, she'd know she was going in the right direction. But nothing stood out to her.

Normally she was very observant. She was good at noticing small details, but yesterday she had been so scared that she hadn't been able to focus on anything. All her concentration had been devoted to keeping close to Marshall. The only thing she remembered seeing was the fuzzy mud. If she could find that, then maybe Chad would be nearby.

She tried to keep track of everything now: tree stumps,

twisted branches, rock formations. There was a tree with several planks of wood hammered into it. She made mental notes of everything she saw so that after she found Chad, she'd be able to find her way back. She stopped often. She'd turn around, and then retrace her steps in her mind.

"Chaaaad!" she shouted.

She didn't have a very loud or strong voice. Ms. Filbert was constantly trying to get her to pro-*ject*. "You have a lot of good ideas, Tamaya. You need to speak with authority." Whenever it was her turn to read aloud in class, everyone always complained that they couldn't hear. And out on the playground, sometimes she'd shout at Monica or Hope, and they wouldn't hear her, even though they were just on the other side of the dodgeball circle.

She tried again, this time putting extra oomph behind it. "Chaa—aad!"

The extra oomph just made her voice crack.

She spotted a tree with white bark and just a few dead leaves left in its branches. One of the branches seemed to be pointing the way back to school. She fixed it in her memory.

A little beyond the tree, she noticed a dark muddy area. There was a layer of scummy fuzz floating just on top of the mud.

She slowly made her way toward it.

She didn't think it was the same mud puddle from the day before. She remembered now that that had been on the side of a hill. The ground around here was fairly level.

She hooked her lunch sack onto a branch, then moved close to the mud. Just like before, there were no leaves on top of the mud, but they had fallen all around it. She knelt beside the edge of the puddle and could feel warmth radiating from the fuzzy mud. Her skin tingled, but that might just have been the heebie-jeebies playing with her mind.

She picked up a leaf, about the same size as her hand. Holding it by the stem, she slowly lowered it into the fuzz. When she lifted it back up, the top half was completely gone. She let it drop, then backed away as she stood up.

She was getting her lunch sack when she saw another puddle of the fuzzy mud just a little farther off. Beyond that, she could see what looked like two more.

She returned to the white tree, its branch pointing the way back to school.

It wasn't too late to go back. If she hurried, she might not get in trouble. She could go see Mrs. Latherly, take the allergy pill, and get her hand rebandaged. Then Mrs. Latherly could give her a note, excusing her for being late to class.

The tree branch pointed one way. Tamaya went the other.

"Chaaaaaaad!" she hollered. This time her voice didn't crack. She continued deeper into the woods.

$$2 \times 65{,}536 = 131{,}072$$
$$2 \times 131{,}072 = 262{,}144$$

20

Three Months Later

In February of the following year, three months after Tamaya went back into the woods to search for Chad, the Senate Committee on Energy and the Environment held a new set of hearings. These hearings were not secret. By this time the entire world knew about SunRay Farm, Biolene, and the disaster that had occurred in Heath Cliff, Pennsylvania.

Dr. Peter Smythe, deputy director of the Centers for Disease Control and Prevention, gave the following testimony at these Heath Cliff Disaster Hearings:

Senator Wright: Were you able to identify this microorganism?

Dr. Peter Smythe: No, not at that time. It didn't match anything in our database.

Senator Wright: Had you or anyone else at the CDC seen this type of rash before?

Dr. Peter Smythe: Again, no. Nor did we know how to treat it. There was no cure.

Senator Wright: And so you ordered the quarantine?

Dr. Peter Smythe: The president ordered the quarantine based on my recommendation. No one was allowed to leave Heath Cliff or the surrounding area. That included our own doctors and scientists. Once they entered the quarantine zone, they could not return. Thousands of people were infected. Five people had already died—the one found in the woods, and then four more who were infected later.

Senator Foote: All because of one little girl?

Dr. Peter Smythe: One week after Tamaya Dhilwaddi went into the woods, more than five hundred people showed signs of the rash, including many of her classmates. But it would be wrong to assume that it was caused by Tamaya. The invading organisms had simply overwhelmed the environment. By the time the first snow fell, this so-called fuzzy mud had spread to lawns and flower beds all over Heath Cliff.

21

A dead tree lay on its side, partially propped up by its broken branches. An image flashed in Tamaya's head of Marshall standing atop a tree that had fallen over. She hurried toward it.

Up close, the tree seemed larger than she remembered. There was a thick branch sticking almost straight up from the trunk, with lots of smaller branches coming off it. She doubted it was the same tree.

Some of the bark crumbled away as she grabbed the base of the largest branch. She pulled herself up, then looked around, just as Marshall had done. Ahead, the ground sloped steeply down to a gully. Rising up from the other side of the gully were two hills.

One of those hills could have been where they'd left Chad. She cupped her hands around her mouth, like a megaphone, and tried to make her tiny voice project across the vast woodlands. "Chaaaaaaaad!"

Her eyes scanned the two hillsides, hoping to see Marshall's rocky ledge, but all she could see were trees and more trees. She hopped down.

The ground went splat beneath her left foot.

Even before she looked, she realized what she had done. She stared down in horror at her left foot, ankle-deep in fuzzy mud. She tried to step free, but her foot wouldn't budge. The mud held tight. She could feel the warmth oozing through her sock.

Her right foot had landed safely, just on the edge of the mud puddle. She took a long stride back toward the fallen tree and grabbed one of the small dead branches. Its rough and pointy edges ripped through her blisters as she desperately pulled with all her might.

The branch broke at the same moment her foot pulled free. She nearly fell backward into the mud but managed to force her momentum sideways and landed on the dry, leaf-covered ground.

She instantly yanked off her sneaker, and then her muddy sock. She now had mud on her fingers, and she wiped them on her sweater and skirt.

She took off her sweater and used it as best as she could to clean her leg and foot. She pulled the cloth back and forth between her toes and continued to rub even after she didn't see any more of the mud on her. She was more worried about what she couldn't see.

She left her muddy sweater on top of the dead tree. Lunch sack in hand, one shoe off, one shoe on, she continued down the slope toward the gully.

"Chaa-aaaa-aad!"

```
2 x 262,144 = 524,288
2 x 524,288 = 1,048,576
```

22

At the beginning of each school year, a parent or guardian of every student at Woodridge Academy was required to fill out a bunch of forms. Among other things, they were to provide the school with their various telephone numbers and emergency contact information.

Those numbers were now being called grade by grade, in alphabetical order. From inside her office, Mrs. Thaxton could hear Mr. Franks and Mrs. Latherly as they made one call after another.

"There's been an incident. . . ."

"Your child is perfectly safe. We're just taking extra precautions. . . ."

"No, we need *you* to personally pick up your daughter.

Your babysitter's name is not in our files. If you want to fax or email your signed authorization . . ."

"No decision has been made yet about tomorrow. We will be sending out a mass email."

Mrs. Thaxton knew she should have been making the calls too, but she couldn't bring herself to do it. She had just gotten off the phone with Tamaya's mother, who had telephoned the school after receiving Mrs. Latherly's message.

No, she had not picked Tamaya up after lunch. Yes, she knew about the rash and was planning to take Tamaya to the doctor, but not until after school. *What's this all about? Where's Tamaya?*

Mrs. Dhilwaddi was on her way home now. Their best hope was that Tamaya had decided to go home after lunch without telling anyone. But they also knew Tamaya wouldn't have done that.

Mrs. Thaxton's chin trembled, and her eyes were blurry with tears. She blamed herself for not putting the school on lockdown the moment she'd heard that Chad Hilligas was missing. She should have done it right then! Better to overreact than to underreact.

But she knew the type of boy Chad was. Whatever had happened to him, wherever he was, she hadn't thought it had anything to do with the rest of the school. Not that she hadn't been concerned about him. She had been very concerned. She just hadn't taken his disappearance as a danger sign for the other students.

She remembered when Chad and his mother first came

to her office. His mother wrote out a check for the tuition, handed it to her, and then, right in front of Chad declared, "He's your problem now."

Tamaya was different. She was the exact opposite of Chad. She was respectful of her teachers and considerate of others. She followed the rules. She was the type of student a teacher might easily ignore, and that, Mrs. Thaxton now realized, might be why she had gone missing without anyone noticing.

Mrs. Thaxton shut her eyes very tight. She knew she needed to be strong in this time of crisis.

Two missing children. Two missing children, in two days.

She did not yet know that a third child would also be discovered missing. She assumed Marshall was safely back in class. Mr. Davison assumed he was still with the headmistress.

No one was worried about *poor Marshall*.

23

The ground was mostly soft under Tamaya's cold bare foot, but she had to step carefully to avoid the sticks and sharp rocks buried beneath the fallen leaves. Her rash had spread the full length of her arm, and she could see small red bumps on her other hand now too. She tingled all over, although she couldn't be sure if that was caused by the mud or by her own heebie-jeebies. It seemed wherever she looked, there were more mud puddles.

Yet, as bad as it was for her, she knew it had to be ten times worse for Chad. At least she'd been able to go home yesterday. She'd been able to take a bath and change her clothes.

"Chaaa—" she started to shout, then gasped and brought

her hand almost to her mouth. Just ahead lay some kind of dead animal, half covered in muck and fuzz. She quickly turned her head away.

It could have been a raccoon, or possibly a small dog. The mud made it hard to know, and she didn't want to look.

She made a wide circle around it, carefully watching every step before gently setting her foot down.

She wondered if there was anybody else, anywhere, who knew about the fuzzy mud. She had tried to tell Mrs. Latherly, but the school nurse had been more worried about peanut butter! Even Marshall hadn't seemed to get it.

Was it possible that she was the only one in the whole world who knew? The thought scared her, but it was also what made her keep going.

If not her, who?

She was determined to make it to the hills on the other side of the gully. "Chaaa-aaad!" she shouted. "Are you out here?"

As the slope of the hill became steeper, she needed to grab onto branches to keep from losing her balance. She bounced from tree to tree, down toward the gully.

There were fewer trees close to the gully, and the ground became even steeper. Tamaya could see down directly into the gully. It was more than half filled with fuzzy mud.

She eased herself into a sitting position and rolled up the top of her lunch sack so nothing would spill. She slid down toward the mud, using her sneakered foot as a brake to keep from going too fast.

The ground was too steep, and she started to turn sideways. She pulled at a clump of weeds to steady herself, but the weeds ripped out of the ground and she flipped over onto her stomach. Her knees scraped across jagged rocks; then her foot slammed into a large boulder, finally stopping her.

She clutched another clump of weeds to try to hold herself in place as she carefully moved her other foot to the boulder for more support. Looking over her shoulder, she saw that she was only a few feet from the edge of the gully. A thin layer of fuzzy scum rose up from it, like smoke.

Not too far away, she could see the flat top of a rock embedded in the dirt. It would make a good jumping-off spot. It looked to be about a six-foot jump from one side of the gully to the other.

She moved, crablike, along the slope toward the flat-topped rock. She dug her fingernails into the dirt to keep from slipping.

She knew she'd have to move quickly. If she hesitated for even a half second, she could end up in the mud.

She pushed herself up, spun around, and slammed her sneakered foot down on the rock. She jumped and hit the other side only inches above the mud. Using her momentum, she scrambled upward, away from the gully.

It wasn't until she was walking again, following a dry creek bed, that she noticed the pain from all the bruises on her hands, arms, knees, and legs. Her shirt had rolled up a bit during her slide, and she had scratches and scrapes on her stomach as well. Still, she knew her pain was nothing compared to Chad's.

"Chaaa-aaad!"

The creek bed wound its way upward between the two hills she had seen from the other side of the gully. She kept looking from one hill to the other, hoping to see Marshall's rocky ledge. Although she knew that even if she found it, that didn't mean Chad was still nearby.

"Chaaaaad!" Her throat was dry, and her weak voice had gotten even weaker.

For a second she thought she heard something. She stopped and listened.

The woods were silent. Looking back the way she had come, she wondered if she'd ever find her way out of there. She didn't want to have to cross the gully again.

She heard a noise. Twigs were breaking, and then footsteps. The steps were uneven, like someone was stomping and staggering.

Then she saw him. He crashed his way through a tangle of twigs and thin branches.

She froze.

"I'm here!" he called, but his voice was little more than a raspy whisper.

He took several deep, uneven breaths, then continued to push his way toward her. "I'm here," he repeated weakly.

His face was a mass of blisters, crusted with pus and dried blood, and so badly swollen, she could hardly see his eyes.

She started to bring her hand to her mouth, then stopped herself, not wanting to get the rash on her lips or tongue.

He came closer. "Where'd you go?" he called from only a few feet away. He sank to his knees. "I'm right here," he whimpered. "Where'd you go?"

She felt overwhelmed with feelings of horror, revulsion, and pity. When she spoke, she spoke softly.

"Are you hungry?"

$$2 \times 1{,}048{,}576 = 2{,}097{,}152$$
$$2 \times 2{,}097{,}152 = 4{,}194{,}304$$

24

The Situation in Heath Cliff (Three Months Later)

Three months after Tamaya found Chad in the woods, Jonathan Fitzman was subpoenaed to testify at the Heath Cliff Disaster Hearings.

Donna Jones, a lawyer from SunRay Farm, was seated by Fitzy's side. Ms. Jones had instructed Jonathan Fitzman never to use the word *disaster*. Instead, he was to refer to it as "the situation in Heath Cliff."

DONNA JONES, ESQ.: There is no evidence of any connection between Biolene and the situation in Heath Cliff.

SENATOR WRIGHT: That is what we are trying to determine. About a year and a half ago, Mr. Fitzman, when you first testified before this committee, you stated that your ergonyms could not live in the natural environment. Correct? You said the oxygen in the air would kill them. Poof.

JONATHAN FITZMAN: That's right. That's what I've been saying. The disaster—I mean, the situation in Heath Cliff is horrible, and I feel really terrible when I think of those people, but it couldn't have been my ergies.

SENATOR WRIGHT: Just to be clear. After you grow these ergonyms, they are combined with other substances and made into Biolene, is that correct?

JONATHAN FITZMAN: There's a lot more to it than that, but I guess that's close enough.

SENATOR WRIGHT: My question is this: Are the ergonyms in the Biolene solution still alive?

DONNA JONES, ESQ.: There is no evidence of any connection between Biolene and the situation in Heath Cliff.

SENATOR WRIGHT: I just want to know, are the ergonyms in Biolene living?

JONATHAN FITZMAN: Yes, that's what gives them their energy. It's their vitality.

SENATOR WRIGHT: And are they still reproducing every thirty-six minutes?

JONATHAN FITZMAN: No. Once they've been congealed in the Biolene, there's no more cell division. Otherwise the ratio would be all wrong. Look, you have to understand, if I thought my ergies would kill someone, I would never, ever have let them out into the world. Biolene is supposed to save mankind, not destroy us.

Senator Wright: Mr. Fitzman, please try not to wave your arms so much. You almost hit your lawyer.

Donna Jones, Esq.: I'm used to it, Senator. I've learned when to duck.

Senator Haltings: I know you've said you have all kinds of safety precautions, but just suppose, Mr. Fitzman—just suppose that some Biolene is spilled. I presume most of the liquid would then evaporate.

Jonathan Fitzman: Yes, and the ergies would disintegrate.

Senator Haltings: But if they didn't die? Would these now free ergonyms be able to start reproducing again?

Jonathan Fitzman: I don't know. Maybe, if they were still alive, but by the time all the liquid evaporated, the air would have already killed them. Any car that runs on Biolene has to be equipped with a vacuum fuel injection system. I'm now working on a way to make sure the fuel tanks remain warm in winter, even if the engine is turned off and a car is parked outside in the ice and snow.

Senator Haltings: You testified last year that an ergonym engages in cell division every thirty-six minutes.

Jonathan Fitzman: Yes, until they've been congealed in Biolene.

Senator Haltings: With trillions upon trillions of cells dividing all the time, aren't there ever mutations?

Donna Jones, Esq.: There is no evidence of any connection between Biolene and the situation in Heath Cliff.

Jonathan Fitzman: You have to understand. Mutations are bound to happen. But that's no reason for everybody to get all freaked out. Normally when cell division occurs, the new organism is an exact copy of the original. But when there's a mutation, that just means there's a defect of some kind. For whatever reason, the copy isn't exact. The defective organism usually cannot survive, and that's the end of it. The rest of the ergies go on doing what they've been doing.

Senator Haltings: But is it possible that an ergonym could have mutated in a way that made it capable of surviving in oxygen?

Jonathan Fitzman: The odds of that happening are, like, a trillion to one.

Senator Haltings: A trillion to one. Okay. Last time you were here, you testified that there are more than a quadrillion ergonyms in a gallon of Biolene. So, a quadrillion divided by a trillion equals a thousand. At a trillion-to-one odds, that would mean in every gallon of Biolene there are a thousand ergonyms that can live in the natural environment.

Jonathan Fitzman: No, that's not right. I'd already factored in the number of mutations when I said the odds were a trillion to one. You're double multiplying.

Senator Haltings: Let's suppose someone spills a few drops of Biolene and all the normal ergonyms instantly go poof. But there might be one mutated ergonym that survives. Then thirty-six minutes later, it will make an exact copy of itself. We'll have two ergies, both capable of living in oxygen. And thirty-six minutes after that, four. And after just one day, there'd be more than a billion of these oxygen-surviving ergonyms. And thirty-six minutes after that, a billion more.

Donna Jones, Esq.: This is pure speculation. I think we can all agree that there has been no conclusive evidence of any connection between Biolene and the situation in Heath Cliff.

SENATOR HALTINGS: What led you to the conclusion that you needed to keep the fuel tanks warm in winter?

DONNA JONES, ESQ.: Mr. Fitzman simply wants to be sure that the people who drive Biolene-powered cars don't have any difficulties.

JONATHAN FITZMAN: You have to understand. I never wanted to hurt anyone.

SENATOR HALTINGS: Unfortunately, a lot of people were hurt.

25

A long line of cars stretched from the front of Woodridge Academy all the way out to Richmond Road, blocking traffic. Many of the mom and dad drivers had tears in their eyes. They hadn't been told the names of the missing children, only that their own children were safe.

At the front of the school, each car was met by a teacher who first verified the identity of the driver, and then went to the proper classroom and escorted the student to the car. These children were often caught off guard and embarrassed by their parents' hugs and kisses.

A uniformed officer kept watch.

It was a slow process, and it had just gotten even slower. There was one car stopped in front of the school that hadn't moved for a long time.

The dad driver who had patiently waited in line so long, silently counting his blessings, had told the teacher who'd come to meet him that his name was John Walsh. He had shown her his driver's license and said he was Marshall Walsh's father. "He's in the seventh grade."

The teacher had smiled at him and said she had known Marshall since he'd been in the fourth grade. "He's a great kid."

Mr. Walsh waited. He watched as other cars pulled up behind him and in front of him. Parents and children were united. The cars drove off, and other cars took their places.

Still, he waited, growing more anxious with each passing second. His hands gripped the steering wheel.

Mrs. Thaxton's voice resounded over the PA system, which could be heard outside as well as in the classrooms. "Marshall Walsh, please report to the office."

Mr. Walsh trembled.

Mrs. Thaxton's voice rang out a second time, sounding a bit more frantic. "Marshall Walsh, come to the office, now!"

A little while later the teacher returned to Mr. Walsh's car, not with Marshall but with a police officer.

26

Tamaya was shaking as she took the juice box from her sack. Using her teeth, she tore the plastic wrapping away from the straw.

Chad, still down on the ground like a wounded animal, rubbed his blistered hands over his arms to try to keep warm. "What are you doing?" he rasped.

"Just hold on a sec," said Tamaya. She had to concentrate very hard to keep her hands steady as she punctured the juice box with the pointy end of the straw.

"Okay, hold out your hand."

She placed the juice box in his hand and felt a rush of revulsion as his fingers touched hers.

She wiped her fingers on her skirt as she watched him

fumble with the straw, and then stick it between his swollen lips.

Chad sucked up all the juice, and continued to suck until the sides of the box collapsed inward.

"You want a sandwich?" she offered.

She removed the lid from the plastic container. It was peanut butter and jelly, with the crusts removed. She thought about what Mrs. Latherly had said, and almost laughed. *Gee, I hope you're not allergic,* she thought.

He sprang at her. She gasped as one hand slammed into her neck. His other hand grabbed her shoulder. She stumbled backward as he ripped the lunch sack from her hand.

The sandwich fell to the dirt.

Chad sat back down. He groped around inside the sack and pulled out a granola bar.

"You didn't have to do that," she told him. "I was giving it to you."

He tore off the wrapping, then ate the bar in three bites.

"You're going to choke if you're not careful," she warned.

"I know who you are," he said as he chewed the last of the bar. "You're Tamaya, Marshall's little friend."

"So? I never said I wasn't."

"You did this," he accused. "I've been thinking of all the things I'd do to you if I ever saw you again, and here you are."

Tamaya bit her lip. "I'm sorry," she said. "I didn't know the mud would make you blind. Anyway, you shouldn't have been beating up Marshall. And you said you were going to beat me up next."

"Don't think I wouldn't," said Chad. "Just because you're a girl."

"The mud hurt me too," Tamaya told him. "My hand and arm are all covered in blisters, and maybe my face too, I don't know. There's something really bad in that mud."

He took several deep, struggled breaths. "Is anyone else looking for me?" he asked. "Do they even know I'm gone?"

"The whole school knows. Everyone thinks you joined a motorcycle gang or something."

He made a noise that could have been a laugh.

Tamaya looked at the sandwich lying on the ground between them. She wanted to pick it up but was afraid to get too close to him.

"The whole time I've been out here," he said, "I've just kept thinking, *No one knows, no one cares*. Over and over in my head. *No one knows. No one cares*."

"Well, your parents have to know," she pointed out.

"Maybe."

"Like when you didn't show up for dinner. Or at bedtime?"

"Yeah, right," Chad said. "Maybe when they came to tuck me in and read me a bedtime story." He made that same distorted laughing sound again, which quickly degenerated into a retching cough.

Tamaya worried he was going to throw up.

The coughing stopped, and Chad took several short quick breaths. "What else you got in here?" he asked, holding up her lunch sack.

"My sandwich is on the ground," she told him. "I'll get it for you, if you promise not to jump at me again."

He said nothing.

She cautiously moved closer, keeping her eyes on him. The two halves had been sliced diagonally. She bent over and quickly picked up one half and then the other.

He remained where he was.

She shook off the dirt the best she could. "Okay, I'm going to hand it to you now. You don't have to grab it."

She held out one half of the sandwich. He reached up, then grabbed her by the wrist, hard.

She didn't make a sound.

He twisted her wrist as he took the half sandwich from her.

"Why are you so mean?" she asked.

He took a bite, and then another without finishing the first. As he continued to chew, she could tell he was having trouble swallowing.

"Sorry there's nothing more to drink," she said. "There's some sliced fruit in the sack."

He dug around in her lunch sack and got the plastic container. He grimaced as he swallowed the last of his mouthful. "This?"

She watched him fumble with the lid.

"You're going to spill it!" she warned, and quickly stepped up and took it from him.

He let her.

She removed the lid and handed it back to him. "Apples and pears."

He ate a slice of fruit, savoring its wetness. He took another bite of the sandwich, smaller this time, then another slice of fruit.

"The jam is homemade," she said, filling the silence. "From real strawberries. It has less sugar than the kind you get in the store. My mom made it."

She didn't know why she was telling him this. She felt stupid.

"It's good," Chad said, to her surprise.

When he finished his half sandwich, she gave him the other half. "Can you see at all?" she asked.

"Only up real close, like just before I smack into something. I can tell something's there, then, bam!" He made the same laughing noise.

He ate a small bite of the sandwich, followed by a slice of pear.

"You must have been really cold," she said. "Did you sleep at all?"

"Who are you, my mother?"

"Sorry for caring," she said.

"I bet you and your family have dinner together every night, don't you?"

It was more of an accusation than a question. She answered anyway. "Just me and my mom. If she's not working too late. My parents are divorced. I don't have any brothers or sisters. My dad lives in Philadelphia."

"Does she read you bedtime stories too?" he asked.

Another accusation.

"Sometimes we take turns reading to each other. She likes to keep up with what I'm doing at school."

She waited for him to say something, to mock her, but he didn't say anything.

He ate the last slice of fruit, then licked the bottom of the container, trying to get every last drop of liquid.

He let her take the empty sack from him. She gathered up the containers and bits of trash and put them all back inside the sack. She was no litterbug.

"No one knows, no one cares," Chad muttered.

$$2 \times 4{,}194{,}304 = 8{,}388{,}608$$
$$2 \times 8{,}388{,}608 = 16{,}777{,}216$$

27

WEDNESDAY, NOVEMBER 3
2:41 P.M.

Marshall banged a stick against one tree, then another, as he wandered aimlessly through the woods. He broke the stick in half and flung the halves in opposite directions.

He didn't know why he did that. He didn't know why he did anything anymore.

He didn't know why he hadn't told Mrs. Thaxton the truth. He didn't know why he'd snuck out of school. He didn't know why he'd returned to the woods.

It certainly wasn't to look for Tamaya. If she wanted to go searching for Chad, that was her problem!

Mostly, he'd just needed to get away. Away from Mrs. Thaxton. Away from his teachers. Away from everybody. If he could have gotten away from himself, he would have done that too.

Nothing made sense anymore. Tamaya should have been glad that Chad wasn't in school. And Mrs. Thaxton acted like Chad was some kind of star pupil. "Did anyone see Chad yesterday? Did you talk to him? What did he say? Where was he going?"

He was going to beat me up, Marshall thought, kicking leaves. *That's where he was going!*

What was he supposed to do, meet Chad on Richmond Road so he could get the snot beat out of him? Would that have made everybody happy?

He kicked a rock, then walked quickly after it, picked it up, and threw it as far as he could.

"Chad's been picking on Marshall all year," Andy had said. "For no reason."

They all knew—Andy, Laura, Cody, everybody. So why didn't anyone do anything? Why hadn't they stuck up for him? Why had they let Chad make his life so miserable, day after day after day?

But that wasn't the real question, and he knew it. The real question was this: Why hadn't he stuck up for himself?

And he knew the answer to that too. Because he was a coward, like Chad had said. "A thumb-sucking coward!"

If Laura thought Chad was mean, then what did she think of Marshall? *Nothing.* He was just a bug that Chad stepped on.

He thought about the way Tamaya used to look up to him, like he was her hero. *Some hero.* When it came down to it, she was the one who had protected him. She'd smashed the mud into Chad's face. And now she was out searching for Chad, because he had been too scared to tell Mrs. Thaxton the truth.

He wondered if Tamaya could possibly be right about the mud. It didn't seem possible. Somebody would have put up a warning sign or something. She'd probably just touched some weird kind of poison ivy.

He stopped. Just ahead, some kind of animal was crouched atop a dead tree trunk, ready to pounce.

Keeping his eye on it, he slowly bent down and picked up a rock.

The sun, shining through the treetops, caused a crisscross of shadows and light over the creature, making it difficult to tell exactly what it was. Possibly a raccoon, or maybe a badger, he thought, although he wasn't sure he knew exactly what a badger looked like. It appeared to be snarling.

Whatever it was, since it was out during the day, it might be rabid.

He rolled the rock over in his hand. "Hey!" he shouted at it.

It didn't move.

He threw the rock toward it, hoping to scare it away. The rock bounced off the tree trunk, and the animal still didn't move.

Marshall picked up another rock and took a few steps closer. "Go away!" he shouted, then took a few more steps.

Maybe it wasn't snarling.

He boldly took another step.

Maybe it wasn't alive.

He moved closer.

Maybe it wasn't an animal at all but just somebody's mud-soaked sweater.

He almost laughed. *Now I'm even afraid of sweaters!*

Beneath the mud, he could see the maroon color and the partially obscured words *Virtue and Valor*.

He realized whose sweater it was.

On the other side of the tree trunk was a large puddle of dark mud covered in a fuzzy scum. He saw a mud-covered sneaker and a rolled-up white sock, also splattered with the mud.

The sock did it.

Something wrenched inside him. All his feelings of shame, self-pity, and self-hatred vanished. He was no longer thinking about himself at all.

"This is really bad," he said aloud.

28

Tamaya held one end of a long stick, and Chad trailed behind, holding the other. "I'm ducking under a branch," she announced, then crouched down, lower than necessary for her, but she had to watch out for him too.

The stick was about six feet long, thicker at Chad's end, with a slight bend in the middle. Tamaya had broken a bunch of twigs off it, but a few of the nubs still remained. She held the cloth sack between her hand and the stick to keep it from rubbing against her blisters.

Somehow, she'd have to get him across the gully. She thought about trying to go around it, but then she might never find her way back to school. Her best chance was to try to retrace her steps exactly.

"I just am," Chad said. "I don't know why. I just know I am."

She had no idea what he was talking about. "You are *what*?"

"You asked me why I was so mean. I'm just saying, it's not like I don't know it."

Tamaya had never expected him to actually answer that question. "Well, if you know you're mean," she said, "then why don't you just stop being that way?"

"I don't know."

"You're not being mean to me now."

"I could. I could just pull the stick from you and hit you with it, even if I couldn't see you. You'd probably scream, and I'd be able to tell where you were. The more you screamed, the more I'd hit you."

"I wouldn't scream. I'd sneak away."

"I'd still probably hit you with it a few times anyway."

"Probably," Tamaya agreed. It was an odd conversation, she realized, but he didn't sound angry, and she didn't feel scared. "But then you'd be left out here, all alone and lost again."

"I know. It doesn't make sense. But that's the kind of dumb stuff I do."

Tamaya thought about what he'd said earlier, about thinking that nobody had noticed when he hadn't come home. "You have any brothers or sisters?" she asked.

"Two sisters and a brother."

"So they would have noticed when you didn't come home?"

"They're perfect," he said, not answering her question. "Good grades, never get in trouble. I'm the only bad one."

Tamaya wanted to tell him that wasn't true, but it was hard to think of something good to say about him. "No one's all bad," she said at last. "The kids at school like you."

"That's just because I'm different. I'm not smart like the rest of you. Half the time I don't get what people are saying. It's like everyone's talking a foreign language. The only reason I go to your school is to keep from going to jail. And it's costing my parents lots of money. That's all they care about. How much money I'm costing them."

Tamaya wondered if he really would go to jail or if that was another one of his exaggerated stories, like the crazy hermit and his pet wolves.

"Sometimes I don't get home until real late," he said. "No one notices. Or if they do, they don't care."

"Where do you go?" she asked.

"Here in the woods. I climb up as high as I can climb, and then just look down at the world. I bring some wood, and hammer it into the trees to make steps. I climb a little ways up, then nail a couple of boards to the tree, and then climb up on them and nail more boards. I always want to get higher."

Talking about his tree-climbing seemed to give Chad more energy. That was encouraging. He'd need all his strength to make it across the gully.

"I saw your tree!" she realized. "It's one of my markers for getting back to school. Follow the white branch, and then turn at the tree with the wood nailed to it."

"That's how I saw you and Marshall," Chad said. "From up there."

He said it like it was something to be proud of, in spite of all that had happened.

Tamaya wondered if he'd also seen the crazy hermit from up in his tree. Maybe that was how he'd gotten the hole in his pant leg too; not from a wolf bite, like he'd said, but from climbing trees.

Thinking about all this, she had momentarily stopped paying close attention, and suddenly looked down to see a puddle of fuzzy mud directly in front of her.

"Stop!" she exclaimed.

Chad took another step.

The stick pushed her forward. She had to hop sideways to avoid the mud, and fell into a tangle of bushes.

"What happened? Are you all right? What happened?"

Twigs scraped her face and arms. "Don't move," she warned. "The mud is right in front of you. Just don't move."

Her hair was caught, and she carefully untangled it as she extricated herself from the bush, still holding on to her end of the stick. "Okay," she told Chad, "you're going to have to try to go around this side of the mud, but there's not a lot of room."

She led him between the bush and the mud, watching every step he took as twigs scraped her legs. "Stay as close to the bush as you can. You have to walk sideways."

He made it safely around the mud, and they continued on down the gully. Fresh scratches covered her arms and legs, but Chad was a lot worse, so there was no point in complaining. "Next time I say stop, you have to stop!"

"Sorry."

"You almost pushed me into the mud."

"Sorry," he said again.

The ground became steeper. Tamaya warned Chad about the gully down below. She knew he was big and strong enough to make the jump. The tricky part would be getting him to a good jumping-off place, and then making sure he jumped in the right direction.

"I can do it," he assured her.

As the ground became very steep, she had to turn around and walk backward. It was like going down a ladder. She gripped the stick tightly with both hands. "Whatever you do, don't let go of the stick," she said.

"I won't."

She directed every step he took. "There's a rock just a little ways down, in front of you. Careful . . . careful . . ."

She watched his foot settle into place as she inched her way backward. "Okay, don't move."

She twisted her neck around. The gully seemed wider than she remembered, and the mud deeper. Just below her there was a rock jutting out from the dirt, above the gully. That seemed like the best place to jump from.

"I'll go first, then you," she told him.

"Okay."

"I'm going to drop the stick now."

"Okay."

She counted in her head. *One . . . two . . .*

On three, she dropped the stick, although she still held her lunch sack. Her feet slid beneath her, but she kept her balance as she spun around and stepped down hard onto the rock.

The rock instantly gave way.

Tamaya tumbled. Her knees banged hard against the side of the slope. She shut her eyes just in time as she somersaulted into the mud.

Her feet hit the bottom of the gully and she forced her head up to the surface. Her eyes remained closed. She could feel the warm muck clinging to her face and over her eyelids. She tried to move, but it was impossible.

"Did you make it?" Chad called.

"No!" she screamed. "I'm stuck!"

She could feel grittiness on her teeth and gums. It tasted like nail polish remover. She tried to spit it out.

"Help me!" she called, then spit again.

"I don't know what to do! What do you want me to do?"

"Get me out of here!"

For a moment Chad didn't respond. Then she heard him, closer than before. "Try to grab the stick!" he shouted.

She stretched out her arms, but there was nothing to grab on to. "Where? Where is it?"

It cracked against the side of her head.

$$2 \times 16{,}777{,}216 = 33{,}554{,}432$$
$$2 \times 33{,}554{,}432 = 67{,}108{,}864$$

29

Tamaya was trapped in a ditch, shouting for help, and Chad was beating her with a stick. That was how it looked to Marshall from the side of the hill.

"Hey, leave her alone!" he shouted, but they were too far away to hear him.

He hurried down the hill, slapping at branches to slow his momentum.

Chad continued to swing the stick like some kind of wild man.

"Leave her alone!" Marshall shouted again.

They still didn't hear him.

When he reached the steep drop-off, he dug the edges

of his sneakers into the dirt and slid back and forth, like a skier, down toward the gully.

"Chad!" he shouted.

Chad stopped midswing.

"If you want to fight someone, fight me!" Marshall challenged.

"Marshall!" screamed Tamaya. "Save me!"

"Drop the stick!" he commanded. He edged his way downward.

Chad continued to swing it. "I'm trying to help her."

"I said leave her alone!"

"The mud's really bad, Marshall," Tamaya called to him. "Chad's blind. He's trying to get the stick to me!"

For the first time, Marshall finally could see Chad's grotesquely blistered and swollen face. *Blind?* He had to turn all his thoughts inside out and backward in order to try to take in what was happening.

"I'm almost there," he called back. "Just quit swinging that stick!" He slid the final few feet to the edge of the gully and then tried to reach out to Tamaya. "I'm here," he said. "Hold out your hand."

She was too far away. "Don't let the mud get on you," she warned.

He didn't care about himself. He let one foot slide down the side of the gully into the mud as he reached for her. The mud was well past his knee when the tips of his fingers touched Tamaya's. Mud pasted her face. Her eyes were shut tight.

"Lean a little toward me," he urged as he inched just a little bit closer.

She bent toward him.

He grabbed her hand. "I gotcha!"

He pulled hard, but she wouldn't budge. "Try to take a step," he urged.

"I'm trying!" she screamed.

It was hopeless. He looked at Chad, standing motionless on the other side. "Chad, we need you."

"I can't," Chad answered.

"You have to," said Marshall.

Chad took a tentative step, then stopped. "I can't," he repeated.

Marshall let go of Tamaya. It took all his effort just to raise his own leg out of the mud. He moved along the side of the gully until he was safely clear of Tamaya.

"Jump toward my voice," he told Chad. "Jump as hard and as far as you can."

"I can't."

"Just do it, you thumb-sucking coward!"

"Hey!" Chad shouted, then came flying toward him.

Marshall grabbed him by the arms as he landed, to keep him from falling backward into the gully. "C'mon," he urged.

He guided Chad back to Tamaya, and they each stepped down into the mud.

Tamaya stretched out her arms.

Marshall grabbed one hand, and Chad found the other.

They pulled.

She still wouldn't move.

"Keep pulling!" Marshall urged.

A deep grunt came from somewhere inside Chad, and Tamaya moved just a little bit closer.

They kept pulling. Another grunt, and Tamaya took a small step. Then another.

"Put your hand on my shoulder," Marshall told her. As she did, he wrapped his arm around her waist and then pried her up and out of the mud.

```
2 x  67,108,864 = 134,217,728
2 x 134,217,728 = 268,435,456
```

30

Marshall took off his sweater and used it to wipe the mud away from Tamaya's eyes. He and Chad had managed to pull Tamaya up the side of the hill to where the ground was less steep. Chad now sat, head down, breathing hard and unevenly.

Tamaya could feel the pressure of Marshall's finger behind the soft sweater fabric as he gently rubbed each eyelid.

"Okay," he whispered to her.

She was afraid to open her eyes.

"I'll get you home, no matter what," Marshall promised.

She listened a moment to Chad's raspy breathing, then allowed her eyes to open.

Marshall appeared blurry at first, but that might have been from keeping her eyes so tightly shut for so long. She blinked. His face was pale and worried.

"I can see you," she told him.

He gave her a small smile.

She took the sweater from him and used it to wipe the rest of the mud off her face, and then her neck and arms. She knew it wouldn't stop whatever was in the mud, but she took comfort in knowing that she'd be home soon. She could take a bath, wash her hair, and go see Dr. Sanchez.

"Here, use this too," Marshall said. He pulled his school shirt up over his head, turning it inside out in the process.

"No, you'll get cold."

"I'm all right."

She took his shirt and used it to clean the inside of her mouth. She rubbed it over her teeth and her gums. She wrapped her tongue with it, then twisted it back and forth.

She cleaned her ears, and then her nose, using her pinky to stick the cloth up each nostril.

"Here. Thanks," she said, but Marshall just put up his hands.

She let the shirt drop.

Chad groaned as Marshall helped him to his feet.

"You okay?" she asked.

"Couldn't be better," he rasped.

She hoped he'd have the strength to make it back. It was already getting dark.

Marshall held Chad's arm as he led him up the hill. Tamaya was on the other side of Marshall.

"You're a good guy, Marshall," Chad said. "Sorry about . . ."

His voice trailed off, and Tamaya was afraid he might pass out, but then he seemed to gather his strength again. "You want to know why I hated you?"

"I already know why," Marshall told him. "You thought I called you a liar."

"You called me a liar? When?"

Tamaya's bare foot stepped on a sharp twig, but she suppressed the pain. The important thing was to keep going.

Marshall reminded Chad about the time he had bragged about riding his motorcycle into the principal's office. "I said, 'No way!' but I just meant it like, 'Wow, that's so cool,' not that I thought you were a liar."

"Oh, yeah, I knew that," Chad said. "I was just giving you a hard time. Besides, I *was* lying. I've never even been on a motorcycle."

Marshall gave a short laugh as he shook his head.

Tamaya knew this was between Marshall and Chad and she should keep out of it, but she couldn't help herself. "Then why'd you hate him?" she blurted. "He never did anything to you!"

Chad took a deep breath, then said something that sounded to Tamaya like *lasagna*.

"What?" asked Marshall.

"Your birthday is September twenty-ninth," Chad said.

"How do you know?"

"And your mom made your favorite dinner."

"Lasagna," said Tamaya. So he really had said that.

"I heard you talking about it at school."

"So?" asked Marshall.

"So, you know when my birthday is?" Chad asked.

He didn't.

"September twenty-ninth," said Chad.

Tamaya was having a hard time trying to put all this together. "And that's why you hated Marshall?" she asked. "Because you have the same birthday?"

"No one cooked me lasagna," Chad said. "No one did anything. You want to know what my dad said? 'Why should we celebrate the day you were born?'"

"That sucks," said Marshall.

"That's still no reason to hate Marshall!" Tamaya insisted.

"I'm not saying it is," said Chad. "I'm just trying to explain, that's all. I figure I owe you that."

Tamaya was trying to make sense out of Chad's logic, when her foot kicked something hard. This time she couldn't suppress the pain. She cried out as she fell onto the leaf-covered ground.

Marshall and Chad stood over her. "Are you all right?"

Her foot throbbed. She hoped she hadn't broken anything. "Man, oh, man," she said as she winced in pain. She took a couple of breaths, and the pain subsided a little bit. "It's just so dark, I can't see where I'm stepping!"

"What are you talking about?" asked Marshall. "The sun's out. There's plenty of light."

Tamaya closed her eyes. When she opened them a second later, the world had gone completely dark.

$$2 \times 268{,}435{,}456 = 536{,}870{,}912$$
$$2 \times 536{,}870{,}912 = 1{,}073{,}741{,}824$$

31

Marshall walked between Tamaya and Chad, an arm guiding each of them. He wore only one shoe, having given the other to Tamaya. It was way too big for her, but she was glad for the protection, even if it flopped a bit with every step she took.

She could still see blurry shapes up close, just like Chad had described, but only if they were right in front of her face. She had lost track of time. She had no idea how far they'd gone or how much farther they had to go.

"Do you know the way?" she asked Marshall.

"I think so."

"Look for a white tree with a branch that sticks out. It points the way back."

"There are a lot of white trees."

"Also a big tall tree with wood planks nailed to it," she told him. "That's Chad's tree. That's how he saw us yesterday."

"I have more than one tree," said Chad. "I climb up one, and then I see one that seems taller, so I climb that one. I want to try to find the highest tree out here."

"That's cool," said Marshall.

"You think? I figured you'd all think it was stupid. Like I was a little kid or something."

"No, that's way too scary for a little kid," said Marshall.

"Too scary for me!" Tamaya agreed.

"You? No way!" said Chad. "You're not scared of anything. I'll take you guys up sometime. There are some boards at the top you can sit on."

Once again, Tamaya could hear renewed energy in Chad's voice as he talked about his tree.

"You can see for miles," said Chad.

For miles? That was nice to imagine, considering she and Chad couldn't even see *for inches*.

Marshall stopped suddenly. Tamaya felt him tighten his grip on her arm.

Chad must have felt it too. "What's wrong?" he asked.

"Shh!" Marshall whispered. "I hear something."

Tamaya listened. It sounded like the scattering of leaves and dirt. Something was moving, some kind of animal, or maybe several animals.

"Chad," she whispered. "When you were up in your

tree, did you really ever see the crazy hermit and his black wolves?"

"I saw a guy with a beard. No wolves."

The sound grew louder. There was definitely more than one animal. A dog barked. It was coming toward them. More barking, from more than one dog.

A dog barked right in front of Tamaya. She cringed, but then Marshall said, "It's not going to hurt you. I think maybe we're rescued."

From a distance, she heard a man's voice call, "They went this way!"

She bent down and tentatively reached out to soft, warm fur. A wet tongue licked her face.

"Oh, don't do that," she said, not wanting the dog to get her rash.

"They're here!" someone shouted, and the next thing she knew there were lots of voices talking all at once. "Are you injured?" "How'd you get here?" "Did someone hurt you?"

"They're both blind," Marshall said. "There's something bad in the mud out here."

She heard what sounded like someone talking on a phone. "We got 'em. All three, two boys and a girl. We're going to need an ambulance. No, they say they weren't abducted, but we'll keep searching."

Tamaya felt a hand on her shoulder. "You're safe now," said a man's voice. "I'm going to carry you back to the school, and then you'll be taken to the hospital."

"Careful. I'm all covered in mud," she warned.

The man chuckled and said, "A little mud never hurt anyone."

She felt his arms wrap around her, and he lifted her up off the ground.

Tamaya was too cold, and too tired, and too sore to try to explain. It was too late now anyway. She let herself sink into his warm wool coat. He'd find out about the mud soon enough. They all would.

As he carried her out of the woods, she asked the name of the dogs.

"The one that you were petting is Missy, short for 'Miss Marple.' We also have Nero, Sherlock, and Rockford. All named after famous detectives."

"'Cause they're good at finding people?"

"They're the best."

"I love dogs," said Tamaya.

32

Turtles

The following is excerpted from the Heath Cliff Disaster Hearings, held three months after Tamaya was carried out of the woods:

SENATOR WRIGHT: Were you able to determine if these organisms were, in fact, the same as the ergonyms that are used in Biolene?

DR. JUNE LEE (RESEARCH SCIENTIST, NATIONAL INSTITUTES OF HEALTH): The DNA is nearly identical, but not exact. We believe that they are a mutated strain of the Biolene ergonyms.

SENATOR FOOTE: But aren't there millions of different kinds of microorganisms living on this planet?

Dr. June Lee: Yes.

Senator Foote: And most of these have never been studied.

Dr. June Lee: That's true. Scientists have identified only about five percent of all the microbes in our biosphere.

Senator Foote: So isn't it possible that the organisms found in the fuzzy mud could have evolved naturally from one of these unknown microbes?

Dr. June Lee: No, that is highly unlikely.

Senator Foote: But not impossible?

Dr. June Lee: Highly unlikely. If it had evolved naturally, then almost certainly it would have adapted to the cold climate.

Senator Foote: What caused the mutation? How did it happen?

Dr. June Lee: I can't say. Every time a cell divides, there's the very small possibility of a mutation. But with billions upon billions of divisions occurring all the time, mutations will happen. It's inevitable.

Senator Foote: How did this supposedly mutated ergonym get from SunRay Farm to the woods of Heath Cliff?

Dr. June Lee: Again, we don't know. A bug, a bird, a wind current—anything could have brought it.

Senator Wright: Even if all you say is true, Dr. Lee, the important question is this: Is the original ergonym dangerous? I'm talking about the one currently used in Biolene, not the mutation. Is it dangerous either to people or to the environment?

Dr. June Lee: No, since the original ergonym cannot survive in oxygen, it poses no danger. But like I said, mutations will occur. As far as what those future mutations may be, I cannot say. But there will be more mutations. That is a certainty.

Senator Wright: Thank you, Doctor, for your testimony, and for your work at NIH. The country is very grateful that you and your agency were able to find a cure for this horrible disease.

Dr. June Lee: Thank you, but actually it was Dr. Crumbly, a local veterinarian, who discovered the cure. We at NIH helped in the testing and mass production, but it is Dr. Crumbly who deserves your thanks.

Senator Haltings: Excuse me, did you just say Dr. Crumbly is a vet?

Dr. June Lee: Animals suffered just as badly as humans. If it weren't for Dr. Crumbly, I suppose in the future the earth would have been ruled by turtles.

33

Frankengerms

The man who rescued Tamaya did find out soon enough. The whole world found out about the mud.

Within hours of the children's rescue, everyone who had been involved in the search began showing signs of the rash: redness, small bumps, a tingling sensation. By the next morning, many of these bumps had turned into blisters, and people awoke to find a mysterious powder the color of their skin on their bedsheets. As it turned out, the powder was their skin, or what was left of it after the mutated ergonyms ate "the good parts."

One week after Tamaya, Chad, and Marshall were found in the woods, there were more than five hundred cases of the rash in the town of Heath Cliff. After two weeks, the number had grown to fifteen thousand.

Many people didn't seek treatment until it was too late. One of the most insidious things about the rash was that there was no pain, just a mild tingling sensation. Normally nerve cells send a pain message to the brain, but the micro-organisms ate through the portion of the cell that transmits the message. It was like a telephone line had been cut. The nerve cells were screaming, "Help! Alert! Danger!" but the brain never got the message.

About the same time that Tamaya, Marshall, and Chad were being loaded into an ambulance, the searchers found the dead body of a person who had been living in the woods, a man with a very long beard.

The three lost children were rushed to Heath Cliff Regional Hospital. Samples of the mud were taken from Tamaya's hair and clothes and sent to the Centers for Disease Control and Prevention in Atlanta, and to the National Institutes of Health in Bethesda, Maryland. Photos of her hand and arm, as well as Chad's face, were emailed to those agencies as well.

The doctors at the hospital searched the medical books and Internet but could find no record of this type of rash. There was no known cure. The best they could do for Tamaya was to keep her extremely clean.

She was thoroughly washed. Her hair was cut off and her

head was shaved. For the next few weeks she was given round-the-clock sponge baths. Every two hours, morning, noon, and night, a nurse would wash her with rubbing alcohol. After each bath she had to rinse her mouth with a special mouthwash. It stung and tasted terrible, and she had to keep it in her mouth for a minute before they allowed her to spit it out. She didn't mind one bit. It tasted strong.

Her mother, and then later her father, came to visit, although they weren't allowed to touch her. She told them she was sorry, but they kept on telling her how proud they were of her.

Later, as the epidemic spread through Heath Cliff, all visitors were banned from the hospital, including her parents. She could still talk to them on her cell phone, which her father had given to her.

Her vision didn't deteriorate any further. If she held her hand in front of her face, she could see it was her hand, but that might have been because she already knew it was her hand. Her doctor tried various other shapes and objects. She could correctly identify a circle, a square, and a triangle, but when he held up a woman's high-heeled shoe, she guessed it was a banana.

She asked often about Marshall and Chad. She heard Marshall was doing fairly well, but she wasn't allowed to see him.

Chad was in very serious condition. That was all she could find out about him. She was told that if he had arrived at the hospital even twenty minutes later, he probably wouldn't have survived.

She never complained. Sometimes, when she felt scared, she'd repeat to herself the ten virtues that she'd been made to memorize at Woodridge Academy: *Charity. Cleanliness. Courage. Empathy. Grace. Humility. Integrity. Patience. Prudence. Temperance.* Partly, she thought that if she was really, really good, then the rash would go away and she'd be able to see again. Deep down, she was also preparing herself for the worst. In case she didn't get better, she wanted to be able to face the world with courage, patience, and grace.

She learned to recognize her different nurses, not only by their voices but also by the sounds they made when they entered her room to give her another sponge bath. Everyone continued to assure her that the best scientists in the country were working on a cure.

Everyone acted so calm and reassuring around her. It was only when she talked to Monica that she found out that the rest of the world was totally freaked out.

"The fuzzy mud's everywhere!" Monica told her. "School's closed. Not just Woodridge. All schools. No one goes outside. I'm not even supposed to talk to you, because my mom's afraid the frankengerms will come through the phone!"

Everyone called it "fuzzy mud," the term Tamaya had used when she'd arrived at the hospital. Even the scientists, who could be seen throughout Heath Cliff dressed in their hazmat suits, called it that. Dr. Humbard, a former employee of Sun-Ray Farm, appeared on all the cable news shows, which was probably why the mutated organisms were now being called *frankengerms*.

The hospitals ran out of room, and schools were turned into rash treatment centers. Cots were set up in the classrooms and cafeterias. Sheets were hung to provide privacy for the round-the-clock sponge baths, administered by dedicated nurses who also wore full hazmat suits.

The president ordered that Heath Cliff and the surrounding area be put under quarantine. No one was allowed to leave, whether or not they showed symptoms of the rash. The airport and railroad stations were closed. The Pennsylvania National Guard patrolled the roads and highways.

34

Miss Marple lay in a crate in Dr. Robert Crumbly's office. Dr. Crumbly stood alongside the crate, a hypodermic needle in his hand. He was glad the poor dog was sleeping. She didn't suffer when she was asleep.

Part Australian shepherd, part chow, and part who-knows-what, Miss Marple used to have thick, gray fur with white, black, and brown spots. Most of her fur had fallen out. Her naked skin was covered in blisters. She'd become deaf and blind.

In her dream, Missy was running through the woods. All senses were on full alert as she searched for the lost children. Leaves flew up as she dashed over them. She barked in joyful triumph and licked the lost girl's face.

To Dr. Crumbly, the triumphant barks of her dream sounded like pathetic whimpers. He carefully opened her crate so as not to wake her.

He worked alone now. Two of his vet techs had come down with the rash, and he'd ordered the others to stay home. He wore gloves and boots but not a hazmat suit. He didn't want to scare the animals.

Miss Marple somehow sensed his presence. Her tail gave a weak thump against the bottom of her crate.

"Hey, girl," he said, and petted the dog, wishing he didn't have to wear gloves. He thought, at the very least, the dog deserved to feel a warm, human touch.

He readied the needle.

Animals suffered from the rash worse than people, since they didn't take baths. It wasn't only dogs and cats. Dr. Crumbly had seen many different infected animals, including hamsters, rabbits, a ferret, and even a skunk named Penelope.

Sadly, he'd been unable to do anything for them except put a final end to their suffering. Over the past two weeks he'd put down more than twenty pets.

There had been one animal, however, that had shown no ill effects from the fuzzy mud. Dr. Crumbly owned a land turtle named Maurice. Maurice had gotten stuck in a patch of fuzzy mud in his backyard, and he'd had to pry him out with a shovel. Three days later, the turtle still hadn't shown any symptoms of the rash.

Peering through the microscope in his small office laboratory, Dr. Crumbly had compared samples of Maurice's skin
with skin samples he'd taken from some of the infected animals. He'd discovered an enzyme in Maurice's skin cell that
didn't appear in any of the other animals' skin cells.

Miss Marple turned her head toward him.

"You're a good dog," he said.

He inserted the needle into her right hind leg, injecting
her with a concentration of the turtle enzymes.

35

Tamaya was the first human test case. Her parents had spoken to the doctor in charge of the experiment, who had cautioned them that just because the cure had worked on animals, there was no guarantee that it would work on people too. Still, what choice did they have?

Tamaya tried not to let her hopes get too high, although she was very glad to learn that Miss Marple had made a full recovery. She loved that dog.

She received two injections of the turtle enzymes each day. Various doctors and nurses were constantly coming into her hospital room to check on her. They always asked her name, which began to bug her after a while. She realized there were lots of other patients and the doctors were very busy, but still, it was a very important experiment. *They could at least remember her name!*

She mentioned that to Ronda, her favorite nurse, who just laughed.

"They know your name," Ronda told her. "They're just testing your memory. Human beings don't normally have these types of enzymes in their bodies, and the doctors are worried about possible bad side effects."

"Maybe I'll grow a shell, like a turtle," Tamaya joked.

Ronda laughed again. "That'd be cute," she said. "And practical," she added.

"Whenever I get tired, I could just duck inside my shell and go to sleep," Tamaya agreed.

Tamaya's other nurses tried to be cheerful and positive around her, but she could tell they were faking it. She didn't blame them. She realized how horrible she must look with no hair and her skin all blistered. But Ronda didn't fake it. She talked and joked with Tamaya like she was just a normal person.

Besides asking her to say her name, her doctors also had her tell them her address and phone number. They asked her who George Washington was. They had her do math problems in her head: five times seven, twenty-six divided by two.

They listened to her heart and lungs. They took her temperature and checked her blood pressure. They made her walk around in a circle and touch her toes.

She began to get better at identifying the various objects her doctor held in front of her face. Still, that didn't mean the treatment was necessarily working. After weeks of practice, her brain might simply have learned how to decipher the blurry images. She also hardly noticed the tingling sensation anymore, but again, that could have been because her brain had learned to block it out.

"How long did it take for Miss Marple to get better?" she asked one of the doctors.

"People and dogs are different," the doctor replied, not answering the question.

She asked him about Chad but was told that Chad had been moved to another part of the hospital. She worried about what that meant.

She slept at odd times, never for very long. She was constantly being awakened, if not for a sponge bath, then for a shot or more tests.

One night, or it might have been during the day, she had a very odd dream. There was a man in her room. He didn't seem to be a doctor, but she didn't know who he was. He said his name was Fitzy.

"That's a strange name."

"I'm a strange person," he said with a laugh.

Every time he spoke, his voice came from another part of the room. He could have just been moving around, but it gave Tamaya the impression of some kind of floating spirit.

"You want anything?" he asked.

"No thanks."

"You sure?" he asked. "When I say anything, I mean *anything*! I'm about to become really rich. Like, the richest man in the world, maybe."

There was a sudden clattering noise.

"What was that?"

"Nothing," he said.

It sounded like he was down on the floor now.

"I just knocked over a jar of those wooden things you stick into your mouth and say *ah*."

"It sounds like you're putting them back into the jar."

"I don't want to make a mess."

"You probably should throw them away," Tamaya told him. "I don't think you should put them in somebody's mouth after they've been on the floor."

"Oh, yeah," he agreed.

She heard them being dumped into the garbage.

"So, can I buy you anything?" His voice was very close now.

"No thanks."

"I don't want anything either," he said. He sounded sad. "You'd think someone with lots of money would want to buy something, wouldn't you?"

"Yes."

"Well, I don't."

His voice was now far away.

"I just like figuring things out. I like science. You like science?"

"It's okay."

"What's your favorite subject?"

"Reading, I guess," she told him. "I like to write too. I think I want to be a writer someday."

"That's good. You can still do that, can't you? I mean, even if you can't see? You can talk into a computer and it will write for you."

"I don't know. I write different than I talk."

"I know what you mean. I think different than I talk. It's like my brain's filled with all these ideas, but sometimes I don't even recognize the words that come out of my mouth."

"You make sense to me," said Tamaya.

"That's good. You sure I can't buy you anything? A piano? A grandfather clock?"

"I just want to get better."

"Me too. I want everyone to get better. I wanted to help people, not start a worldwide epidemic."

He sounded very sad. Tamaya wished there were something she wanted. "Oh, I know!" she suddenly remembered. "I need a new school sweater."

She woke up sometime after that while Ronda was giving her a sponge bath. She thought about her dream and laughed.

"What's so funny?" Ronda asked.

"Nothing." *A grandfather clock? A piano?*

The sponge bath felt nice.

Often, she didn't know if her eyes were open or shut. It was something she had to think about. She opened them now.

The world was full of light and color. Ronda had red hair and dark eyes. The walls were yellow.

Tamaya started to tremble.

"What's wrong?" Ronda asked.

Everything still looked very blurry, but it was a well-lit blur.

"Tamaya, are you okay?" Ronda asked again.

She was afraid she might still be dreaming. She spoke tentatively, almost afraid that if she spoke, the world would go dark again.

"Ronda, I can see you," she said, and when the world didn't disappear, she trembled even harder. "I can see."

Ronda began shaking too. She hugged Tamaya very hard, which was against the rules.

"You need to call your mother!" she declared. "I'll get the doctor. You call your mother!"

She hugged Tamaya again, and then got her cell phone for her from the table by the bed.

"What time is it?" Tamaya asked. "Are you sure it's not too late?"

"It doesn't matter what time it is," Ronda said. "Call her now!"

• • •

At three-forty-five in the morning, Tamaya's mother was startled awake by the ringing of the phone. Instantly her heart filled with terror. It took all her courage to answer it, as she tried to prepare herself for the worst.

"Yes?"

"Hey, Mom, guess what?"

36

Snow

Two days later, the first snow fell. Tamaya still couldn't make out the individual snowflakes, but she was able to see zigzagging streaks of gray and white outside her hospital window.

It was beautiful. The whole world looked beautiful to her, even the bright green Jell-O that came with her lunch, with coleslaw magically suspended inside.

Ronda led her onto the outdoor patio next to the cafeteria. Wearing a ski hat over her closely cropped hair, she lay on the cement and caught snowflakes with her tongue.

It snowed for four straight days. Tamaya learned that Marshall had begun getting Dr. Crumbly's injections and that he was showing great improvement. Nobody seemed to know anything about Chad, and she was afraid to push it, afraid what she might find out.

Her doctor gave her large black-framed glasses that were too big for her face. Seeing him clearly for the first time, she nearly fainted. With soft brown eyes and curly hair, he was even cuter than Mr. Franks.

"I get all flustered and tongue-tied when he looks at me," she told Monica over the phone. "It's a good thing I didn't know what he looked like before. Everyone would have thought I had all kinds of horrible side effects. I probably would have forgotten my own name!"

Monica laughed.

"You don't sound so scared anymore," Tamaya noticed.

"I know. I think it's all the snow. I mean, I know the mud's still there, underneath, but everything just seems safer. And I'm just so happy you're almost all better!"

Tamaya could hear a crack in her best friend's voice. It sounded like she was crying. Tamaya started to cry too. Then they both laughed at the fact that they were crying. They stayed on the phone a while longer, crying and laughing at the same time.

One day in late December, Tamaya's doctor was checking her pulse while she watched television.

A TV set hung from the ceiling in the corner of her hospital room. She could feel her heart rate quicken at his touch. She hoped it didn't throw off his measurements.

Her TV program was interrupted by a breaking news story from Heath Cliff, Pennsylvania. Her doctor let go of her wrist and picked up the remote. He raised the volume.

A man was standing in the back of Woodridge Academy, near the edge of the woods. He was surrounded by news reporters. The bar across the bottom of her TV identified him as Dr. Peter Smythe, deputy director of the Centers for Disease Control and Prevention. It felt odd watching something on TV that was happening right at her school. Snow was falling outside her hospital window, and she could see it falling on the man on TV. Tamaya thought he looked more like a lumberjack than a doctor. He had a thick bushy beard and held a shovel.

The man dug his shovel through the snow, and then, with his bare hand, reached down and pulled out a big glob of black goo.

"Fuzzy mud," he said. Ice crystals stuck to his beard, and Tamaya could see his frozen breath as he spoke. "I'm holding in my hand more than a billion of your so-called frankengerms."

Tamaya felt all tingly again, watching him hold the mud just like she had once held it.

"And I'm happy to report that every last one of them is dead," the man said. "The organism cannot survive subfreezing temperatures."

Tamaya and her doctor looked at each other. *Could this really be true?*

Several of the reporters applauded, and Tamaya could hear cheers coming from other rooms in the hospital.

"Does this mean the crisis is over?" a reporter asked.

Before Dr. Smythe answered, the bar at the bottom of the TV screen had already proclaimed CRISIS OVER! FRANKENGERMS ALL DEAD!

Tamaya wondered how they could know for sure. Maybe the frankengerms were just hibernating, like bears.

"How do you know they're not simply lying dormant?" a reporter asked, almost as if she were channeling Tamaya's thoughts. "How do you know they won't wake up again when the weather turns warmer?"

"We've examined them in our labs. I've personally looked through a microscope and seen the disintegrated membranes. I assure you, they will not *wake up.*"

Still, Tamaya wondered, how could he know they were *all* dead? Maybe somewhere beneath all that snow, there was one that was still alive.

"Of course, the CDC will continue to monitor the situation," Dr. Smythe said. "Although extremely unlikely, it is possible that another mutation could have occurred. Somewhere out here there may be one mutated ergonym capable of surviving the freezing cold. We'll know more after the snow melts."

$$2 \times 1 = 2$$

37

The quarantine was lifted.

Under the direction of the National Institutes of Health, Dr. Crumbly's cure was mass-produced. It successfully treated more than sixty thousand people and animals afflicted with the Dhilwaddi Blister Rash—the now official name of that particular medical condition. Medical books were being updated with before-and-after photos of Tamaya Dhilwaddi's skin.

Two weeks after being discharged, Tamaya and Marshall returned to the hospital, this time as visitors. Tamaya brought jars of homemade strawberry jam, belated Christmas presents for her doctor and nurses. Marshall carried a plastic food container.

Tamaya still wore glasses, but Monica had given her new ones for Christmas. The frames were neon green and semi-transparent. Monica told her they were *très chic,* French for "very stylish."

Tamaya's hair had begun to grow back. She wore a pink cap over what she called her fuzzy head. She had some scars on her hand and arm, which her doctor said would fade. There was a pockmark on her face, which her friend Summer insisted only made her prettier.

"In order to be perfect, everyone woman needs an imperfection," Summer had told her.

This sounded like an oxymoron to Tamaya, but it was still nice to hear.

After Tamaya gave the strawberry jam to Ronda, Ronda said she had something for her too.

She handed her a flat box. Tamaya opened it to find a new school sweater.

"How'd you know?" She couldn't remember ever telling Ronda about the sweater. "You shouldn't have. It's way too expensive."

"It's not from me," Ronda explained. "The box arrived here for you yesterday. I've been trying to figure out how to get it to you."

Tamaya discovered a small card, which read, *For a girl of extraordinary virtue and valor.* It was signed *Your friend, Fitzy.*

"Who's Fitzy?" Marshall asked, reading over her shoulder.

"I thought I dreamed him," Tamaya answered, mystified. "Good thing I didn't ask for a piano!"

"What?" asked Marshall.

Chad Hilligas was one of the few rash patients still in the hospital. The skin on his face had been so badly damaged, he had been put in a ward usually reserved for severe burn victims.

The door opened as Tamaya knocked. "Hello?" she said as she entered. Marshall was no longer with her.

Chad was sitting up in bed, wearing green pin-striped pajamas. A ray of sunlight shone through the window, highlighting a shaft of dust particles and casting a glare across his heavily scarred face. He wore a pair of the hospital-issued black-framed glasses.

Tamaya was happy to see the glasses. If he'd been blind, there would have been no need for them.

"Tamaya!" he said.

She was afraid he might hate her again, because of what she'd done to him, but he seemed glad to see her.

"Hi, Chad." She set down her sweater box, then stuck her hands into the back pockets of her jeans. "How are you doing?"

"I'm not supposed to move my mouth too much," he said, keeping his face noticeably still as he spoke. "They had to take skin from another part of my body and put it on my face."

"Oh," said Tamaya. "You still look like you," she assured him.

"Just call me Buttface," he said.

She was shocked. "You mean they . . ." She covered her mouth with her hand. "At least you think it's funny. Instead of being all mad and everything."

"Nothing makes me mad," he said. "It's weird. Ever since I could see again, the world just looks a lot better than it did before."

"I know what you mean," Tamaya agreed. "Everything's beautiful."

"I hope it lasts," said Chad.

"Me too," said Tamaya.

She wasn't sure if Chad meant he hoped the world lasts, or if he hoped it continues to look beautiful. Either way, she agreed with him.

The door pushed farther open as Marshall backed his way into the room. He turned around, holding a tray with three plates of lasagna.

"The nurses let me use the microwave."

"Happy birthday!" exclaimed Tamaya.

Chad didn't say anything. He stared at the food, then looked from Marshall to Tamaya, and back to Marshall.

"He's not supposed to talk," Tamaya told Marshall, then quietly whispered, "His butt was transplanted onto his face."

Chad pulled back his covers, then slowly slid down from the bed. He stepped toward Marshall, who set down the tray and nervously backed away.

It might have been all the talk about frankengerms, but with his scarred and rigid face, and his now outstretched arms, Tamaya thought Chad looked a little bit like the Frankenstein monster.

Marshall backed up against the wall. Chad clasped Marshall by the shoulders, pulled him close, and hugged him.

"Thanks, man," Chad said.

Marshall twisted free. "It was Tamaya's idea."

Tamaya laughed at Marshall's awkwardness. She wondered why boys were always so weird about hugging, but then her heart stopped when Chad's eyes fixed on her. He opened his arms wide and said the same three words he'd said to her once before.

"You're next, Tamaya."

38

Courage, Humility, and Grace

The following testimony is excerpted from the transcript of the Heath Cliff Disaster Hearings:

> **Senator Haltings:** So when you returned to the woods to look for Chad, did you see more of the mud?
>
> **Tamaya Dhilwaddi:** Yes. Just about everywhere I looked! But there could have been more of it the first day too. I just didn't know to look for it then.
>
> **Senator Wright:** Please speak directly into the microphone, Tamaya. We're having trouble hearing you.
>
> **Tamaya Dhilwaddi:** Sorry. I said, the first time I went into the

woods, I didn't know about the fuzzy mud, so I wasn't looking for it. All I could think about was wanting to get out of there.

Senator Haltings: Because it was against the rules to go into the woods?

Tamaya Dhilwaddi: But I wasn't allowed to walk home alone either.

Senator Haltings: Hobson's choice.

Tamaya Dhilwaddi: I don't know what that is.

Senator Haltings: Hobson's choice. It's when you have to choose between two options and they're both bad.

Tamaya Dhilwaddi: Yes, they were both bad.

Senator Wright: Well, Tamaya, speaking on behalf of this committee, we are very glad you chose to follow Marshall into the woods. The two of you may have saved the world.

Tamaya Dhilwaddi: But everyone got the rash because of me.

Senator Wright: No. From everything the scientists told us, that would have happened anyway. Maybe a week or two later. And by then it would have been too late to contain it.

Senator Haltings: The quarantine wouldn't have been in place. Someone could have stepped in the fuzzy mud, gotten on a plane, and flown to Los Angeles, or Paris, or Hong Kong. We could have had a worldwide epidemic, and in places where the temperature never drops below freezing.

Senator Wright: Thanks to you, Marshall, and Chad, the country got an early warning.

Senator Haltings: You're a very brave young lady, Tamaya.

Tamaya Dhilwaddi: I wasn't brave. I was scared. Marshall's the brave one.

Senator Foote: So how does it feel to have a disease named after you?

Tamaya Dhilwaddi: It's a great honor . . . I guess?

Epilogue

For hundreds of thousands of years, human beings lived in a world without Biolene. There was no gasoline, no nuclear power plants, and no electric lights. Water was clean, and the night sky glittered with a million stars.

There were also fewer people in the world.

It is estimated that a thousand years ago, there was a total of about three hundred million people living on earth. World population didn't reach the one billion mark until the early 1800s. But by the 1950s, that number had more than doubled. In 1951, more than two and a half billion people inhabited the planet.

By the 1990s, world population had doubled yet again. And in 2011 it was reported that there were more than seven billion of us eating, drinking, driving cars, using bathrooms, day after day after day.

$$2 \times 7,000,000,000 = 14,000,000,000$$
$$2 \times 14,000,000,000 =$$

Which is why, even after the Heath Cliff Disaster, the Senate Committee on Energy and the Environment voted unanimously to support the continued production of Biolene. The committee was presented with a Hobson's choice: either risk worldwide catastrophe or give up on a source of clean, affordable energy. They concluded that the risk of catastrophe was extremely small.

They hoped.

Jonathan Fitzman assured the committee that there would be new safety procedures. This included taking daily samples from the storage tanks in order to test for oxygen-tolerant ergonyms. If even one such ergie was found, all the "little fellows" inside the tank would be destroyed.

Soon, Biolene-powered cars and trucks would fill the highways. SunRay Farm would establish new farms in Michigan, Idaho, and New Mexico—sites chosen either for their cold winters or for their lack of vegetation. Scientists determined that the frankengerms had thrived as well as they had because of all the organic material in the woods. The ergies were especially fond of freshly fallen leaves.

• • •

One week after returning from Washington, DC, Tamaya still felt a glow of excitement from the experience. Everyone had told her how well she'd done, praising her maturity and poise. Monica kept reminding her that she was famous.

It was scary returning to the woods again. It was scary climbing up Chad's tree, especially wearing clunky snow boots and fat gloves. Chad in front, and Marshall right behind, both promised they wouldn't let her fall. She didn't dare look down.

The climb, the cold, and her fear of heights left her short of breath but also exhilarated when she reached the cross boards that Chad had nailed into place.

"Isn't it great?" Chad beamed.

"Awesome!" Marshall agreed.

Tamaya held tight to the tree as she looked out across the frozen woodlands. The world was so beautiful. She just hoped it would stay that way . . . after the snow melted.

Tamaya Dhilwaddi
Room 308
Heath Cliff Regional Hospital
December 9
Late Assignment

How to Blow Up a Balloon

1. You start with a flat balloon. (The color doesn't matter.) You want to fill it with air from your lungs.
2. Look for the knobby end. If you stick your finger through it, your finger will be inside the balloon. But don't stick your finger in there!
3. Okay, put the knobby end inside your mouth. Your lips should be tight around the knob so that when you blow, all your air will go into the balloon and not around it.
4. Okay. Hold the balloon between your first and second fingers. You have to hold it loose enough to allow air in, but tight enough so that it doesn't move.
5. Now blow.

6. Repeat step five until the balloon is full.
7. Between blows, you will need to take breaths. Be sure to squeeze your fingers tight around the balloon when breathing in, so that the air can't escape.
8. Okay, now you have to tie the balloon. That's the hardest part! Tightly hold the balloon between your first and second fingers so that no air gets out. There will be a little dangly piece of your balloon left over. Stretch out that part and wrap it once around your finger. Then tie it into a knot by slipping the knobby end between your finger and the part wrapped around it.
9. Remove your finger. Ta-da!

About the Author

LOUIS SACHAR is the author of the *New York Times* #1 bestseller *Holes,* winner of the Newbery Medal, the National Book Award, and the Christopher Award. He is also the author of *Stanley Yelnats' Survival Guide to Camp Green Lake; Small Steps,* winner of the Schneider Family Book Award; and *The Cardturner,* a *Publishers Weekly* Best Book, a Parents' Choice Gold Award recipient, and an ALA-YALSA Best Fiction for Young Adults book. His books for younger readers include *There's a Boy in the Girls' Bathroom, The Boy Who Lost His Face, Dogs Don't Tell Jokes,* and the Marvin Redpost series, among many others.